The Theft & the Miracle

REBECCA WADE

The Theft & the Miracle

Katherine Tegen Books
An Imprint of HarperCollins*Publishers*

www.harpercollinschildrens.com

Library of Congress Cataloging-in-Publication Data
Wade, Rebecca.
    The theft & the miracle / Rebecca Wade. — 1st ed.
        p.   cm.
    Summary: Overweight with acne-prone skin, twelve-year-old
Hannah always feels unsure of herself, but when a wooden
statue of Jesus goes missing from the cathedral, she discovers a
special connection with both the statue and a larger force.
    ISBN-10: 0-06-077493-2 (trade bdg. : alk. paper)
    ISBN-13: 978-0-06-077493-6 (trade bdg. : alk. paper)
    ISBN-10: 0-06-077495-9 (lib. bdg. : alk. paper)
    ISBN-13: 978-0-06-077495-0 (lib. bdg. : alk. paper)
    [1. Statues—Fiction. 2. Artists—Fiction. 3. Conduct of
life—Fiction. 4. Self-confidence—Fiction. 5. Cathedrals—
Fiction. 6. Supernatural—Fiction. 7. England—Fiction.]
I. Title. II. Title: Theft and the miracle.
PZ7.W118213The 2007   2006000822
[Fic]—dc22   CIP
                                                              AC

Typography by Christopher Stengel
1 2 3 4 5 6 7 8 9 10
❖
First Edition

For Björn

❖ CONTENTS ❖

The Theft & the Miracle

✦ CHAPTER ONE ✦

JACOB MARTIN

It was in early November that the news began to reach the city. Not that anybody took much notice at first. Life was hard enough here, with the scurvy, leprosy, food shortage, and crippling taxes following the recent disastrous harvest. There was no point in bothering with some new trouble, especially one so far away as Dorset.

Then one mild, wet market day in the middle of the month, a peddler arrived from Gloucester with a sack of knives for sale. That evening he shared a flagon of wine and a salted herring pie with a little group of local tradesmen at the Black Bear on the corner of St. Peter's Street. They were glad to have a newcomer bringing tidings from another part of the country.

But the news the peddler brought filled them with dread. A terrible sickness had attacked the southwest ports, and was spreading across the map of England like a dark and evil stain. Now it had reached Gloucester and was less than thirty miles off! There, the man told them, the churchyards overflowed with new graves, and there were not enough men left to bury the dead, who were either flung into great pits or left to rot where they lay, continuing to spread the fatal corruption even after life had departed.

The peddler's story was soon widely known, and fear began its stealthy journey around the city walls. Strangers were no longer welcomed but treated with suspicion, or even turned away altogether. Neighbors became distrustful of one another. The city was no longer cheerful, bustling, noisy, but sullen, brooding, watchful.

At last, one day at the beginning of December, a woman burst into the cathedral during Mass and begged the monks to come and bring the Sacrament to her dying husband. The monk chosen to accompany her took one look at the sick man and fled.

That night the man died. The bishop ordered that his blackened and swollen corpse be buried secretly, by night, hoping that it was an isolated case and the people of the city might never know that they had harbored a victim of the Black Death. But within a week the monk who had fled began to shake with a high fever, and an ugly dark swelling appeared under his arm. Four days later he was laid to his final rest in the monks' cemetery. By the middle of that month eighteen more deaths had been reported, all bearing the horrifyingly unmistakable signs of the disease.

Now the terrible plague was among them; it was no longer a vague rumor from a distant town but a hard fact, with freshly turned earth in the churchyard to prove it. Doctors were powerless to cure or prevent the infection, and the clergy were mostly too afraid for their own lives to give comfort to the sick and dying.

One man was unaware of the fear and distrust spreading as rapidly as the disease itself, and this was because for four weeks he hadn't spoken to a single soul. Jacob Martin was old, sick, and gradually dying of starvation, but his eyes still burned as brightly as when he had been a young apprentice fifty years ago.

Late one afternoon toward the end of December, he sat alone in the attic room of a half-timbered house in a narrow, evil-smelling alley that ran alongside the north wall of the monastery stables. It was bitterly cold in the room. He had no money for fuel; he had had barely enough for the single candle that inadequately lit his workbench, and when that burned down he would have nothing but the darkness and the numbing cold as companions. The need to finish the statues obsessed him. While he worked he forgot that he was hungry, that he was tired; he forgot everything except the task before him.

At last he sat back, exhausted. Gouges, files, chisels, and rasps covered the scored and battered workbench; he didn't need them now, would never need them again. He thought sorrowfully that he had no son to give them to, no apprentice who would use them; there had been apprentices, of course, but none who had lasted long. Jacob Martin demanded a dedication and passion for his craft that he had never found in any of the young boys sent to him for instruction, and it was too late now.

The Virgin and Child were carved from a single piece of oak, but were unjoined. For infants cannot remain always attached to their parents, and one day this baby would leave his mother and grow to be a young man, and at last . . . For a few seconds it seemed to Jacob that the shadow of the Cross passed over his beloved figures, and the eyes of the mother were filled with a sadness that he had not put there. Then the illusion passed. The Virgin gazed into the eyes of her Child with an expression of tender astonishment, the baby returning his mother's loving smile with delighted infant laughter.

He closed his eyes, remembering that warm, bright day the year before last when he had ridden out from the city in the spring sunlight in search of firewood. But the little gray mare had seemed to have other ideas. When she led him to the ancient hillside with its crown of oak, he knew at once that this was no place to gather firewood. A dull wash of low cloud stained the sky above the grove of trees, and the sound of birdsong that had provided such cheerful accompaniment to his journey was now stilled entirely. Silence wrapped itself around him like a shroud, chilling his bones. This was a holy place. A terrible place, from which the sun itself had fled to escape the taint of old ritual that hung still in the air, like smoke from sacrificial fire.

Then he saw it. The huge white oak lying newly felled by the spring storms; a great warrior chief surrounded by his shocked and grieving army. The tree was surely dead, cruelly severed at the base of the trunk, yet the spirit still hovered, waiting, waiting for the moment of rebirth.

And today it had life once more, the wood new-fashioned by the file and the rasp. Jacob felt a profound sense of release. His life's work was over and he could die with a quiet mind.

But now fatigue and hunger made him weak. With difficulty he stood up, took his three remaining coins from a stone jar on the empty hearth, grasped an earthenware pitcher on the bench, and slowly made his way down the rotting wooden steps to the cobbled street below. A fresh fall of snow made the ground slippery and treacherous and twice he stumbled and almost fell, but at last he reached the little group of market stalls and ramshackle dwellings that huddled up against the monastery wall, like chicks clustering around a mother hen. The stench of rotting fish lying on the greasy cobbles was mixed with the powerful smell of animal skins coming from Tanner's Lane, and the filthy river water added its own particular quality to the pungent air.

A penny bought him a newly baked loaf of rye bread; the remaining two he spent on weak ale to fill his pitcher, not trusting the water from the city well, which was as often as not contaminated by the dung from the assorted animals that roamed freely and occasionally had to be shooed from the cathedral itself.

Returning, he noticed a young woman and her baby crouched against the monastery wall, sheltering from the icy wind. As he approached them the woman looked up, her eyes dull with hunger and tiredness. The baby stirred fretfully and gave a sharp, shrill cry. Jacob bent down and set the jug of ale on the ground beside them, placing the loaf above it. With difficulty, because his old arms were stiff, he took off his threadbare cloak and placed it carefully around the woman's shoulders so that it covered her child as well. Then he slowly climbed the narrow steps. Although he had no supper now, he could still feast his eyes on his finished work.

But Jacob never saw his Virgin and Child again. As he reached the top of the steps, a terrible faintness overcame him and a searing pain gripped his chest. He pitched forward, clutching at the stair rail, and collapsed, lifeless, on the wooden platform. This was where the landlord's wife found him when she came to collect the rent the following morning.

The woman went straight to the cloisters to tell

the monks the old man was dead, for it was common knowledge that he was working on an important commission for the cathedral, and she was eager to remain in favor with the monastery. It could provide them with a new tenant, perhaps.

Two monks were immediately dispatched to the attic workshop, their cowls pulled tightly around their faces. As they approached the door, the elder of the two turned to his companion.

"There is nothing to fear from this house," he said softly. "Jacob Martin perished from want of food and physick, not from the pestilence."

Then, at the same moment, both men caught sight of the completed carving, which stood just as Jacob had left it for the last time. They gazed in silence.

The younger man was the first to speak. "It is fine, is it not, brother?"

"It is more than fine." The older man turned his head away. His mouth was set in a hard line, and the olive skin of his face had turned pale. "It is possessed," he muttered, under his breath.

"And the money?"

"What of money?"

"The commission. It has not been settled."

"The old man has no need of money now."

"But his family? Will they not claim what is due?"

"He had no family. The work was to be paid for upon completion. Not a penny was to be given for his labor till then. The church has no obligation."

The two men looked toward each other and smiled slightly. Then, remembering their office, they looked grave and departed.

So it was that on the twenty-fourth of December, thirteen hundred and forty-eight, while the monks observed the eve of the Feast of the Nativity and the Black Death stalked the country-side all around, the cathedral gained the statues of the Virgin and Child for nothing.

But from this moment, in the city itself, the disease lost its power.

Jacob Martin had given more than the statues. He had given his own life.

CHAPTER TWO

THE STORM

To BEGIN WITH, THE ONLY ODD thing about Friday, October the twenty-eighth, was that the weather forecast was wrong.

"Today will be bright and windy, with temperatures a little below average for this time of year," the man on the radio had said at breakfast time.

But by two o'clock in the afternoon all the lights were on in classroom 8B at Manningham School; the air was warm despite the open windows, and the sky outside was a dirty, yellowish gray, the color of a fading bruise.

Miss Millicent Murdoch drew herself up to her full height of five foot two, tucking in a strand of long gray hair that had escaped from the knot at the back of her head. Her chin receded slightly beneath a long, pink-tipped nose, giving her the look of an anxious mouse.

"I want you to imagine a man with two left hands and one right," she announced.

Class 8B considered this remote possibility in weary silence. They were used to this kind of thing from Mad Millie.

"He has five pairs each of black, green, and red gloves, and he wants to be sure of selecting two left and one right of the same color," went on Miss Murdoch bravely. "How many gloves must he take from his drawer before he can be certain he has the right combination?"

"Is he blind, Miss Murdoch?" enquired Sophie Brown politely.

"As well as having three hands?" asked Matthew Cole, rather less politely.

Miss Murdoch took a deep breath. "I think we must assume there has been a power outage and he is in the dark," she said firmly.

There was a distant rumble of thunder and the lights went out briefly, as though trying to set the scene.

"Then why does it matter what color his gloves are if no one can see them?" called out Sam, who was very good at math and enjoyed confusing

Millie Murdoch, though she needed no help from him.

"You mustn't take this too literally," she said, beginning to sound slightly desperate. "It's only a math problem! Now, he has thirty gloves of three colors. If we call each color 'x,' that means x equals three. So to be sure of two left and one right, he would have to take out . . . ?"

"Nineteen," said Sam promptly.

Miss Murdoch closed her eyes briefly, then continued as if there had been no interruption. "He must take out all the right-handed gloves plus two of at least one color, which will of course be 6x plus 1. That is because 10x is the total number of gloves, so 5x is the number of right- or left-handed gloves. In this case, however, we must say right. . . ."

Hannah tried hard to concentrate on what was being said, then sighed and gave up the struggle. She was hopeless at math on the best of days and today wasn't the best of days. She had woken up to discover that she had gained another two pounds, and a large red pimple on her nose. Her math homework had been returned to her with "See me after school" written in red ink, and the close, stifling weather was giving her a headache.

She gazed discontentedly out of the window.

Why couldn't she be beautiful like Emily? Or clever like Sam? Or good at sports like Sophie? Or funny like Matthew?

"If he adds 1x plus 1, he must get at least two left-handed," Miss Murdoch's voice twittered on.

In fact why couldn't she be absolutely anybody except fat, pimply, boring Hannah Price?

The class grew restless. Pencils were dropped. Chairs scraped on the floor. A light murmuring began. Thunder rolled again, slightly closer this time, and Hannah continued to gaze out the window.

She noticed how the odd, lurid light made the goalposts on the playground stand out harshly against the somber sky; she saw how the line of elms in the field beyond was so sharply outlined that the trees seemed closer than they really were; she observed the peculiar quality of gray that made storm clouds so different from any other kind. Her hand itched for her pencil.

Hannah Price was different from everyone else at Manningham School, but it wasn't because she was overweight, or had bad skin, or was useless at math. The thing that made her different was that she noticed things other people didn't. And once she'd noticed them, she knew how to draw them.

"However! If he has sixteen, he could have got fifteen right and one left . . ."

Reluctantly, she turned back to the classroom and gazed longingly at the clock on the wall, but it said only two fifteen. It had to be later than that!

Miss Murdoch chattered on brightly, illustrating her remarks with minute, mouselike figures on the blackboard that nobody could see except herself.

At last the bell rang for the end of the class, and before leaving, the teacher gave them their homework, which was to draw a graph showing how the problem could be solved most efficiently.

"My mom says she can never understand why she ends up with so many odd socks," said Susie. "I wonder if I should get Millie Murdoch to explain how it happens with the aid of a graph."

Hannah looked at her watch, puzzled. It said two forty.

"The clock must have stopped!" She turned to Sam, who was putting away his books.

"Yeah. It stopped when the lights went out."

"But the lights came back on again."

He shrugged. "Must've been on a different circuit."

"I thought that lesson was never going to end! Did you get what she was saying?"

"Mm. All stuff we did last term. Stupid old thing makes it look like rocket science. They should've retired her years ago."

"Can you give me a hand with the graph? Kind of explain it very slowly, like I was a retarded five-year-old?"

His thin, freckled face broke into a grin. "All right. We could go and see that new movie that's on at the Odeon tomorrow afternoon, then my mom can give us something to eat afterward and we'll do the graph."

Hannah blushed with pleasure. She hardly ever got asked to do anything on the weekends. "We could see if that new girl with the glasses wants to come to the movie," she said. "Jessica something-or-other. She doesn't seem to have made many friends yet. You okay with that?"

"Sure. And I'll pay for the movie. I've got cash." He winked at her.

She didn't like to enquire too closely into the state of Sam's finances, but she took the wink to mean that the family was for some mysterious reason in funds at the moment. Sam's father seemed to divide his time pretty well equally between being at home out of work, and doing time at the city jail for housebreaking. Whether he was inside or not didn't seem to make much difference to the family fortunes; in fact the Fallons were often suspiciously better off just after Arthur had been sent down for a stretch. At the moment, Hannah knew, he was inside, which might account for Sam suddenly having cash.

On the face of it Sam Fallon and Hannah Price had absolutely nothing in common except that they were the same age and went to the same school. The odd thing was that ever since their first day, something between them had clicked. When she was with him, Hannah forgot that she had acne and surplus fat; not because Sam was too polite to mention these things—Sam was never polite to anyone! He just didn't seem to notice.

"Come on!" he said. "Last lesson of the week. Art. Now's your chance to make the rest of us feel like retarded five-year-olds!"

Normally, this was the best moment of the week for Hannah, but today she felt tired and listless, and her headache was getting steadily worse. The atmosphere in the art room was heavier than ever and the thunder, though still distant, was almost continuous.

The class was divided into pairs, to draw portraits. Hannah found herself paired not with Sam, as she'd hoped, but with Emily Rhodes. That was all she needed! Emily was tall and slender with long blond hair, a flawless, honey-colored complexion surrounding a straight, delicate nose, a small neat mouth, and wide, slightly slanting green eyes. And she was clever. One of the most brilliant students in the class, destined for one of the top universities. Admittedly she didn't seem to come from a background where there was much money, as her school uniform, though always clean and carefully pressed, had a slightly threadbare, mended look, but for some reason, far from detracting from her prettiness, this only seemed to accentuate it. It wouldn't have been so bad if Emily hadn't always been so terribly nice to Hannah—then she could have hated her quite cheerfully. As it was, whenever she got anywhere near her, her body seemed to grow to twice the size and her personality felt as if it were shriveling up, like a dead fly in a tub of lard. But there was one small crumb of comfort. Although Emily was beautiful and better at absolutely everything else than Hannah, she wasn't quite so good at art.

"I'm afraid I don't seem to be getting a clear picture of your bone structure," Emily said now, apologetically.

"That's probably because it's invisible. My face is too fat."

Emily frowned and shook her head. "Oh dear!" she sighed. "This is so hard. You'll just laugh when you see it."

"Look, don't worry about it," said Hannah, scowling. "I'm not exactly an artist's dream model. Just do me a favor and leave out the pimple on my nose. Okay?"

"Sure. Though my dad always says you should draw what you see, not what other people want to see."

"I suppose that's honest, at least."

"Being honest doesn't necessarily put food on the table!" Emily smiled wryly. "It certainly never put any on ours."

Hannah looked at her curiously. "So your father is an artist?"

"Yes." She went on drawing, glancing at Hannah every now and then. "Not a very successful one, I guess."

So that explained the frayed, carefully preserved school uniform.

"Well, you'll be different. You're so smart you'll never be short of money! You can be a doctor, or a lawyer like Tabitha's dad. Her family is really rich."

Hannah glanced in the direction of the girl sitting just behind them.

Tabitha Trelawney was striking rather than beautiful, with glossy black hair and very pale skin, large dark eyes made even more dramatic by black eye shadow and a strong, slightly sulky mouth. Ever since her arrival at the school the previous year, several of the other girls had copied the eye shadow, dyed their own hair black, and adopted a lot of white face makeup, with the result that nearly half the girls in 8B now looked as though they suffered from some mysterious illness. Hannah smiled to herself and turned back.

"I don't want to be a doctor or a lawyer," replied Emily quietly.

"Well, a banker then. You've got the head for it. You're good at math."

"I don't want to be a banker either."

"Well, what do you want to do then?" Hannah looked at her with interest.

"I want to be an artist."

Hannah stared at her in disbelief. "But why?" she blurted. "You've already said there's no money in it. You know that from your father. Besides, you could do anything! You don't need to choose something you're—" Less good at, she'd been about to say but she stopped herself just in time.

"I'm not going to be like my father," said Emily. "I'm going to be famous and successful. I'm going to paint what people want to see!"

And when after ten minutes she turned the easel around, Hannah saw a face that was still quite recognizably her own, though subtly altered. It wasn't just that her acne had miraculously disappeared; her nose was very slightly narrower, and there was a faint suggestion of definition to the chin and cheekbones. The eyes were the same size and shape, but the lids and lashes had been darkened, which made them seem bigger, and the mouth was straighter and more regular. But what struck Hannah most forcibly was the almost complete absence of expression. It was, she thought, a face without *attitude*. Well, maybe she'd been more successful than she'd thought in trying to disguise the surprise she'd felt on hearing that Emily wanted to be an artist!

She smiled. "Thanks, Emily. Definitely an improvement on the original."

"You could do the same with a little makeup," Emily replied kindly.

"And six months' dieting!"

"Perhaps not quite six months."

Hannah gritted her teeth, removed the picture of herself, clipped a fresh sheet of paper to the easel, and prepared to draw Emily. She began by taking a long, close look at her subject. Then she took out her pencil. She worked steadily and in silence, forgetting everything except the task in front of her. For twenty minutes she even forgot how she felt about Emily, who sat quite still, without speaking. She seemed to be staring at a spot just behind Hannah.

At last Hannah sat back and examined the portrait critically. She was pleased with the lines of the face, the shape of the chin, the pretty curve of the upper lip. Something about it wasn't right though. She had always considered Emily to be beautiful. Now she wasn't quite so sure.

She looked up to see the art teacher standing at her shoulder.

"That's very good, Hannah," said Miss Beamish thoughtfully. "Very good indeed."

"Something's wrong though, isn't it?" She frowned in an effort to see what it was. She looked back to Emily, who now appeared serene and lovely as always, and Hannah was struck by how vividly green her eyes were. It was impossible to show that with only a pencil of course, so what was the matter with her drawing? There was something about the expression that she didn't understand.

"I can't see anything wrong," said Miss Beamish. "Come and see what you think, Emily."

Emily got up and walked round to the other side of the easel while Hannah watched carefully to see her reaction. She noticed that her expression changed very slightly when she saw what Hannah had drawn, and the odd thing was that now it seemed she had gotten the eyes right after all.

Miss Beamish was looking at the picture of Hannah. "Very nice, Emily," she said, smiling. "But you have left out something that makes Hannah's face special."

"What?" An uncharacteristic flush momentarily darkened the honey-colored skin.

"Her personality."

Hannah blushed in embarrassment and looked down at the floor, but the awkward situation was mercifully saved by the bell, which signaled the end of the class.

The students left quickly, eager to get home for the weekend, and Hannah found the new girl, Jessica, in the coatroom, where she suggested going to the movie the following day. Jessica looked surprised but pleased and they arranged to meet outside the cinema at two o'clock.

Then she remembered that before going home she had to see Miss Murdoch about her math homework. She took her time packing her book bag and walked slowly to the staff room, half hoping that Miss Murdoch wouldn't remember to wait for her.

However, when she got there she found not only the math teacher but Mr. Henderson, who taught geography, with Tabitha Trelawney. He seemed to be discussing a piece of homework with her and the two of them looked up briefly as Hannah came in.

Miss Murdoch greeted her enthusiastically. "I wanted to see you, Hannah, because I feel you are still very confused about these equations and I think you and I should get together after school one day next week to really come to grips with the problem and clear your mind of the fog!"

Hannah couldn't help thinking that any help from Miss Murdoch was only likely to make the fog thicker, but she found herself saying thank you and agreeing to visit the teacher's house the following Thursday afternoon for some extra tutoring. Then, blushing as she noticed Tabitha's eyes raised toward her, and thinking that now it would be common knowledge that Hannah Price was so useless at math that she needed special help, she escaped to the coatroom, put on her coat, and made her way to the entrance hall, where, after a few seconds spent arguing with her conscience, she bought a Mars bar from the vending machine. It had been a bad day, she told herself. She needed something to cheer herself up on the way home.

Although the air was now stiflingly close, the storm still hadn't broken. Most people had already left, but Katie Brown, a small, pale girl who looked as though she didn't get enough to eat, was standing by the front door peering up at the purplish and threatening sky.

"Where's your coat, Katie?" asked Hannah, as Katie seemed to be preparing to leave in just her sweater and skirt.

"Can't find it," replied Katie unhappily. "I had it this morning, but when I came down at lunchtime to get some money out of the pocket, it was gone!"

Hannah looked at her in alarm. "So what did you do for lunch?"

"Nothing. I didn't have any."

"What? You must be starving!"

Katie nodded miserably and Hannah reached resignedly into her pocket.

"Have a Mars bar," she said. "At least it'll stop me from getting even fatter!"

Katie took it and immediately started to unwrap it. As she ate, a faint color returned to her cheeks.

Hannah went back to the vending machines, inserted another coin, and waited for the heavy clunk that told her a can of Coke was waiting in the tray at the bottom. She picked it up and handed it to Katie, who was starting to look more cheerful.

"Maybe someone took your coat by mistake when they went outside at lunchtime and accidentally wore it home. If they left theirs behind, you could take that instead. Let's go and take a look."

But a quick glance around the coatroom, though showing plenty of abandoned clothes strewn on floor and benches, didn't reveal a spare coat.

"How far have you got to go?"

"Linton Green."

"That's quite a long way, isn't it? Which bus do you get?"

"The ninety-three, but my bus pass was in my coat pocket."

"I'll lend you some money and you can pay me back tomorrow." Hannah felt in her pockets, but discovered that after paying for the Mars bar and the

Coke, she now had only ten pence. That wouldn't get Katie as far as the end of the road.

"Tell you what—you'd better take my raincoat. It'll be far too big for you but at least it'll keep you dry. Don't forget to bring it back on Monday though, or my mother will kill me!"

"Thanks, Hannah." Katie took the coat and put it on.

Hannah giggled. "It's nearly down to your ankles! The hood's zipped inside the collar. You're going to need it any minute, though."

"What about you? You're going to get soaked now."

"I've got my pass, and the bus stop's only the other end of Tanner's Lane. I'd better run, before the rain gets going."

Hannah watched Katie retreating like a sleeping bag on legs and set off in the opposite direction at a brisk trot. But before she had gone far, there was a deafening clap of thunder as the storm broke directly overhead, and a minute later she could hardly see where she was going for the blinding downpour.

CHAPTER THREE

THE STATUE

THERE WAS NO POINT in trying to reach the bus stop now—she would just have to try to find a place to shelter until the worst of the rain had passed. There were no shops nearby, only the vast, towering cathedral, loftily impervious to the sudden storm. It had seen far worse than this in the last nine hundred years.

Battling against the driving rain and strong wind, Hannah reached the end of the north wall and came to the beginning of the wide gravel path that led up to the great west door. She could just make out that a smaller door inside it stood open. She ran with difficulty along the deep, loose gravel, stepped over the sill of the larger door, and stood dripping on the enormous mat.

Immediately the noise of rain and traffic ceased, and she was struck by the sudden hush. There was a sort of stillness that held itself quite aloof from the soft murmur coming from the visitors, who walked sedately, inspecting stone tablets and gazing up at the vaulted ceiling. It was very cold.

There was a smell of ancient stone and timber, of dust and candle wax. She breathed in slowly, enjoying the strangeness of it, then sneezed violently. This attracted the attention of a man wearing a black cassock, who ambled over in her direction, a friendly look on his face. She noticed that he had a small white tag pinned to his chest, with the words "Day Chaplain" written on it.

"Strange how many turn to God when the weather's bad," he observed, winking at her.

Hannah felt herself blushing. "I . . . just came in to see the Virgin and Child," she said with an attempt at dignity, trying to make it sound like it was something she did regularly.

"Go ahead then—they're waiting for you," said the chaplain. "But you won't find them down that aisle," he added, as Hannah set off purposefully toward the other end of the cathedral.

"Oh." She stopped and turned. "Have they been moved then?" She was still trying to make it seem as if she had a better reason for the visit than simply keeping out of the rain.

"Not for the last four hundred years or so," he replied equably. "Before then I couldn't say. Try up there."

Hannah admitted defeat and followed his direction slowly down the north aisle, passing a tomb where the stone effigy of a medieval knight lay, hands crossed on his chest, sword reaching down to daintily pointed toes. She glanced up at the great north window, but she wasn't able to make out the stained glass with the day so dark outside and couldn't remember what story it told. She passed the strange modern signs that seemed to be warnings against exploding lunchboxes but in fact were only forbidding flash photography, and came at last to the end of the aisle, to the left of the altar. There stood the ancient figures of the Virgin Mary and the Infant Jesus, for which the cathedral was famous all over the world.

Hannah couldn't see the statues immediately, as a small crowd of Japanese tourists was looking at them respectfully and obediently not taking photos. She sat down in a pew to wait, near a man who was leaning against a pillar and fiddling with the spokes of an umbrella. She shivered as the damp seeped through her thin clothes. At last the little group moved away, and Hannah found herself alone with the figures.

They were smaller than life-size. The Virgin stood at a height of about four feet, holding a baby that was in fact a separate figure, able to be removed and put back in its mother's arms, just like a real baby. The Virgin gazed at her Child with an expression of devoted and almost bewildered tenderness, while the baby looked straight back into her eyes and smiled happily.

Hannah hadn't set foot in the cathedral since that time six years before when she had come with the rest of her class on a field trip. She remembered how one of the boys had reached out to stroke the Virgin's hair and a different chaplain, a lady that time, had been very angry with him and told him not to touch the statue because she was so old and special and it was disrespectful to go putting sticky fingermarks all over her. Somehow Hannah had gone away with the impression that the Virgin didn't like small children much, which didn't really make sense when you thought about it.

But now that she was older and had a chance to see the statues alone, she was struck not only by how astonishingly beautiful they were, but also by an overwhelming sense of friendliness that seemed to radiate from the small couple.

She reached into her book bag, pulling out her sketchbook and a pencil. Something made her want to capture the expressions on those faces for herself. Slowly she drew a few tentative lines and, gaining confidence, settled to her task with absorption.

Then something very strange happened. Quite suddenly she found herself growing warmer. The chill left her fingers and they began to tingle, as if she were sitting in front of a hot fire. At the same time she felt the pencil grow firm and quick and deliberate. It traveled with complete assurance, tracing the soft, gentle eyes, the protective, encircling arms, the long, flowing folds of the robe, the baby's outstretched fingers.

Hannah had no idea how long it took her to complete the sketch. It could have been twenty seconds or twenty minutes, but at last her pencil stopped moving and she sat back, exhausted. Sweat broke out on her forehead and she felt sick and faint. She unwound her scarf and threw it down. Then she closed her eyes.

"Feeling all right?"

She looked up to see the chaplain standing anxiously over her.

"Yes—yes, I think so. I suddenly felt faint."

"Put your head down then—that's right. Better now? Good! Strange place to faint—it certainly can't be the heat. Seems even colder in here than usual! May I see your drawing?"

Hannah took her hands off the page and looked down at the finished sketch. She stared in disbelief. *It was quite perfect.* Every detail of form and expression was represented, down to the last fingernail.

"That's remarkable!" The chaplain's voice seemed to come from a long way away. "I was watching you. You came in here only ten minutes ago and as soon as you sat down, you were scribbling away like someone possessed! You did that in less time than it takes to write a shopping list. You're quite an artist, young lady!"

Hannah said nothing. She was still staring at her drawing.

"Well, well, artist or not, you'd better be getting home and out of those damp clothes before you catch pneumonia. I think you'll find the rain has stopped now."

Hannah put the sketch carefully in her bag and got unsteadily to her feet. She still felt weak with shock. With shock and with something else. She had an odd sense of being somehow dislocated. As though she were standing looking at herself from a great distance. A distance that seemed to have another dimension than just space. Briefly she felt that time, usually so well behaved and predictable, which marched obediently to the demands of clocks and calendars and history books, suddenly had become shifting and shapeless, like a thick mist appearing from nowhere, treacherously concealing a friendly and familiar landscape.

She picked up her bag and carefully made her way to the main door of the cathedral, where the man with the umbrella was standing and looking speculatively up at the sky.

When she got outside she felt slightly better. The fresh air cleared her head and she found that the chaplain had been right—it was no longer raining, but the clouds still hung low and heavy over the darkening city and the wind, which half an hour earlier had been so violent, had dropped entirely. Even the rush-hour traffic seemed muted and distant.

She didn't have to wait long for a bus, and the journey passed in a confusion of vague, disturbing thoughts. When she got off, she walked the short way home, glancing every now and again over her shoulder to reassure herself she was alone.

❖ CHAPTER FOUR ❖

THE DRAWING

"HANNAH, WHERE ON EARTH have you been? Dinner was ready half an hour ago! We were worried about you! And where's your coat?"

"Sorry. When I got out of school, it was about to rain and Katie had lost her coat so I lent her mine and then I went and sat in the cathedral till it stopped."

As usual, her mother went straight for the weak spot in her reasoning.

"If it was raining, why did Katie need your coat any more than you?"

"Her bus pass was in her pocket, so she had to walk and she lives in Linton Green."

"But why the cathedral? It's the last place I'd have chosen! Why didn't you go into a café or somewhere warm? That's such a damp old place. You'll be lucky if you haven't caught a cold! Anyhow, come and eat now."

"What's for dinner?"

"Stir-fried vegetables with brown rice."

"Sounds healthy. Anything for dessert?" she asked hopefully.

"Fresh fruit salad. And you can have low-fat yogurt on it if you like," her mother added generously.

Hannah sighed. "Thanks."

When she had finished eating, she went into the sitting room to talk to her father.

"Hello, sweetheart, what have you been up to?" He was tapping away at the computer and didn't turn around.

"Oh, the usual. You know. English, French, chemistry."

"Good, good."

"P.E. was awful."

"Mm."

"Art was okay."

"Of course. Good!"

"And then this afternoon we helped a blind man with three hands find his gloves when the power went out."

"Good . . . good . . . Good God! What?" He stopped tapping and turned around in alarm.

"He wasn't a real man. Just someone thought up by Miss Murdoch."

"Who is Miss Murdoch?"

"She teaches math. You've met her before on parents' night."

"Have I? Can't remember, I'm afraid." He smiled and shook his head, then seemed about to go back to the computer.

Hannah began to feel slightly desperate. She needed his attention.

"Dad," she said, "what do you know about the Virgin and Child? I mean the ones in the cathedral."

William Price wasn't an insensitive man—he just found it hard to concentrate on the things which didn't particularly interest him. There were two things about this question that interested him. The first was that it was about history, which was the subject he taught at the university; the second was that he noticed an edge to his daughter's voice which struck him as unusual.

He pressed Save and turned all the way around in his chair to look at Hannah thoughtfully.

"Only what everybody knows. World famous,

mid-fourteenth century, carved from local oak, once supposed to have had miraculous powers, mysteriously survived the wholesale destruction of religious images during the dissolution of the monasteries. Generally considered to be one of the finest examples of medieval wood carving in Europe. But you knew all that already, surely?"

"Yes . . . I suppose so. I never thought about it much, though. Do you know any more?"

Her father nibbled his thumb for a moment before replying.

"As a matter of fact there is something that always struck me as curious. Historically speaking, that is. The cathedral records seem to show that the statues made their first appearance sometime around the end of thirteen forty-eight. Now if that's true, the Black Death was just beginning to take a hold on this part of the country by that date. The odd thing is that from thirteen forty-nine onward, there were very few cases of the disease recorded in the city itself and those that did get it apparently brought the contagion from elsewhere, yet often survived when they came here."

Hannah frowned in an effort to take in all this information.

"So . . . what are you saying, Dad? That the statues

somehow protected the people of the city from the plague?"

"I'm not saying anything. Historians are supposed to weigh evidence, not jump to exciting conclusions. But it's always struck me as an interesting coincidence, and there's no doubt that people flocked to the cathedral for several centuries afterward because they believed the Virgin and Child had power to cure their ills."

He stopped being a history teacher suddenly and became a dad again.

"You still haven't told me why you want to hear all this."

"Oh well, I'm probably imagining things, but it's just that today it was raining at the end of school and I went into the cathedral to wait until it stopped and, well, something weird happened, Dad. Something really weird."

"Tell me."

Hannah explained as best she could about the sketch. When she had finished, her father said nothing for a moment or two. Then:

"May I see your drawing?"

She fetched her book bag from the hall, took out the sketch, and handed it to him in silence.

He looked at it carefully, then got up and took

down a large, illustrated volume from the bookcase. After a few seconds he found the page he was looking for and laid Hannah's drawing next to it while his glance moved from one to the other. At last he closed the book and handed back the sketch.

"It's very good," he said in an odd voice. "Very good indeed. In fact, it's—" He stopped himself, but Hannah finished the sentence for him.

"Too good? It's okay, Dad, you can say it. You're right, it is. But I know I did it, because one of those chaplain people watched me and he was curious because he said it hardly seemed to take me any time at all." She tried to say the words calmly but couldn't quite stop them from shaking.

Her father heard the fear in her voice. "What do you think happened?" he asked gently.

"I've really no idea. I just wanted to keep out of the rain!"

He smiled. "Well, there's probably no point in trying to explain it now. We may just have to accept that we have a genius in the family! In any case, you've always been very good at drawing—it's not as if this were a complete fluke."

"Hm." Hannah glanced at her watch. "I should do some homework." She stood up, took the sketch, and walked slowly out of the room.

Her father watched her go, but he didn't return to the computer. Instead he reopened the book with the photograph of the statues and sat gazing at the page in thoughtful silence until his wife came in twenty minutes later and switched on the TV for the news.

❖ CHAPTER FIVE ❖

MRS. ABBOTT

SATURDAY MORNING'S SKY had the clear, blue-eyed innocence of a child who has quite forgotten yesterday's tantrums. The red and yellow leaves of the beech tree outside Hannah's bedroom window sparkled in the autumn sunlight, and her mood matched the weather. Something good was happening today. What was it? Of course! She was going to see a movie with Sam.

She had a leisurely shower, weighed herself (the scale was equally depressing no matter which foot she stood on), put on jeans and a sweatshirt, and went downstairs.

Her parents were sitting at the kitchen table with a pot of coffee between them and the weekend papers.

Hannah poured cereal into a bowl, added milk from a carton on the table, and sat down.

"Doctors are predicting a bad flu epidemic this winter," remarked her father from behind the newspaper. "It says those most at risk will be the very old and the very young."

Hannah swallowed a mouthful of cereal and suddenly clapped a hand to the side of her head. "Oh no! That reminds me! I promised I'd go and visit old Mrs. Abbott this morning."

"But you went to see her last Saturday," protested her mother. "Isn't it someone else's turn this week?"

Hannah nodded. "Susie was supposed to go, but she's got her cousin staying for the weekend, so I said I'd go instead."

Her father raised an eyebrow. "Do your friends avoid Mrs. Abbott, or has she just taken a particular shine to you?"

Hannah shook her head. "She likes Susie best, but she complains about all of us. Trouble is, she's got agra, agra—"

"Agoraphobia?"

"That's it. Means she's scared to go out. So since Mr. Abbott died, someone has to do her shopping for her and go to the post office and run errands and things."

"And that someone's generally you?" said Dad with a smile.

"Oh, someone's got to go and visit the old bat, I suppose, even if she does treat you like something that's gone bad at the back of the refrigerator."

"Well if you're going, you'd better hurry," said Mom, "or you won't be back in time to have any lunch before you go out again."

She finished her breakfast, seized a couple of shopping bags, and ran out of the house.

Mrs. Abbott lived about three quarters of a mile away and Hannah walked fast, hoping the old lady wouldn't have an endless list of things to do that would make her late for the movie.

Number 43 Heliotrope Gardens shared an outside wall with its semidetached neighbor, number 45, but the two houses seemed equally eager to insist they shared nothing else.

Mrs. Abbott's side had been painted a dark green about thirty years earlier and never repainted since, while next door changed color so frequently that even the postman got confused and had to check the number on the gate before delivering. Where number 43 had plain net curtains with dingy, dark-red mock velvet at each side of the sagging bow window, number 45 had an elaborate canary-yellow blind, pleated and scalloped, with a lacy white lining. It looked as if someone had hung up an enormous piece of frilly underwear.

Walking up Mrs. Abbott's path, Hannah noticed that the two or three hopeless-looking pansies in her window box had been flattened by yesterday's storm. As she rang the bell she glanced next door and saw a red-and-green garden gnome leering at her from behind a plastic birdbath. She leered back at it.

"I thought the other girl was coming today." Mrs. Abbott opened the door so suddenly that Hannah almost fell into the house.

"I'm sorry, but she couldn't after all." She wondered why Mrs. Abbott always managed to make her feel guilty before she'd even set foot inside.

"Now, since you're so late, you won't be able to bring back the potatoes in time for me to boil them for my lunch."

"It's only eleven o'clock, Mrs. Abbott."

"I daresay some folk eat their lunch anytime, but I like mine on the table by twelve sharp!"

That was the thing about old people, reflected Hannah. They seemed to need routine to feel safe. Mrs. Abbott never went out, never entertained, never needed to please anyone except herself, but she lived her life according to a strict timetable that would have made air traffic control look slack.

"Now you're here you can change that light-bulb for me." She pointed to the small but hideous chandelier that hung from the middle of the hall ceiling.

Hannah went and fetched one of the kitchen chairs and placed it under the light. She climbed up and unhooked the little chains that held the glass pendants so she could take out the old bulb. The old lady handed her a new one.

"But this is only forty watts," said Hannah in surprise. "Don't you need something a bit brighter for the hall?"

"Brighter just means more expensive. You don't catch me wasting money on the electric bill!"

After replacing the bulb with difficulty because the socket was old and rusty, Hannah hooked the chains again, climbed down, put the chair back, and picked up the shopping list from the kitchen table.

"Just a small cauliflower. I don't want to be eating it till Christmas! And when you're choosing the apples, don't get Granny Smiths this time. My teeth can't handle them."

She fetched an ancient wallet from the mantelpiece and rather reluctantly handed it over. "And don't forget to count the change!"

Hannah set off wearily. She hated shopping for Mrs. Abbott, especially at the small grocery store, because the old lady usually wanted only two or three of anything and it all had to be weighed separately. The owner got irritable and the other customers impatient.

At last it was all done. She quickly ran through the list. Small cauliflower, two carrots, four potatoes, an onion, three apples, one can of tuna fish, small tub of margarine, small box of tea bags, small loaf of white bread, and a pint of milk.

When she got back, she unpacked the shopping, put it away, gave Mrs. Abbott back her wallet and asked if there was anything else that she needed, hoping the answer would be no.

"That'll do," said the old lady. "And thanks. It was kind of you to come." This was said in exactly the same tone of voice that she usually said everything else in and at first Hannah thought she must have misheard. Mrs. Abbott never said thank you to anyone as far as she knew. Suddenly she was filled with pity for the lonely old woman, who could neither go out nor bring herself to welcome outside help.

"That's okay, Mrs. Abbott," she said. "I'll see you again next week."

Then she left before she could regret her promise.

CHAPTER SIX

AT HOME WITH THE FALLONS

WHEN SHE GOT TO THE ODEON, Sam and Jessica were already waiting for her.

"Thought you'd forgotten," he said.

"Sorry, I had to do community service work this morning and I was late getting back. Hi, Jessica. How come you never get involved with that kind of thing anyway, Sam Fallon?"

"I've got my own scheme. It's called prison visiting, and I like to keep it in the family!" He grinned, but Hannah felt a pang of guilt. She'd forgotten for a moment about Sam's dad.

The movie was fast-moving, noisy, and full of special effects, but for once she couldn't concentrate. She felt restless and uneasy for some reason, and kept glancing behind her in the flickering half darkness of the cinema.

"That bit about Vulcatron was great, wasn't it?" said Jessica as they emerged, blinking, into the sunlight.

"Which one was he?"

Sam stared at her in disbelief. "Vulcatron was the planet they were attacking, you dope! What movie were you watching?"

"Sorry," she muttered. "Must have missed that part."

"I'd better get home now," said Jessica. "Thanks for asking me along. I'll see you on Monday."

She walked toward the bus stop and Sam and Hannah set off in the opposite direction.

The Fallons lived on the first floor of a block of apartments near the station. It was the unfashionable, run-down end of the city, and the block itself was shabby and in need of renovation, but the Fallons' apartment was a little oasis in a desert of dereliction. The windows sparkled, and the front door was proud with fresh paint. Sam's mother was waiting for them.

Eve Fallon was small and slim with short, shiny black hair. Today she was wearing a short black skirt and a bright yellow blouse. She looked like a cheerful little blackbird.

"Hello, Hannah, my love!" Eve beamed at her. "Long time no see! I keep asking Sam when he's going to bring you over, but he always says you're too busy with your homework and your drawing. Really wonderful you are with that pencil of yours, he says! Now you take a seat, dear, and I'll bring the food soon. And what do you two think you're staring at? Mind your manners!" This was said to Jack and Jessie, six-year-old twins, who were watching Hannah from behind the sofa, wide-eyed, thumbs in their mouths.

Hannah sat in an armchair and began to feel better. It was such a friendly room, and as usual it gleamed with cleanliness. Every surface was dusted and polished, the mirror sparkled, and the chair covers looked like new. In fact, she didn't think they had been there on her previous visit.

"Have you got new chair covers since I was here last, Mrs. Fallon?" she asked.

"Oh, yes!" replied Sam's mother with pride. "What do you think?"

"They're very nice." Hannah blinked slightly at the huge scarlet roses that lay against a background of brilliant white.

"And just take a look at my new TV!"

Hannah had no chance of missing this. It was

the most enormous set she had ever seen, and completely dominated one end of the room.

"So things aren't too bad when Mr. Fallon's, um, away?" As soon as she had said this she wondered if it sounded rude, and regretted it, but Mrs. Fallon didn't seem at all bothered.

"Things are a good deal better when Arthur's inside," she said decidedly. "Not that I don't miss him of course, in a way. But at least when he's there he can't drink his way through the child-support money. And of course there's the cash I get from the cleaning work I do. Five ladies I've got now and they all pay very well, I'm glad to say."

Hannah had a suspicion that this didn't quite account for the sudden display of prosperity, but after all, it was none of her business where the Fallons got their money from.

She got up to help but was firmly made to sit down while Sam's mother brought pizza from the oven, sandwiches from the fridge, jelly roll, lemon sponge, and finally a large plate of chocolate brownies. Hannah was relieved that her mother wasn't there to count the calories.

Mrs. Fallon herself hardly seemed to eat anything, but she made sure Hannah's plate was never empty.

After they ate, Sam showed Hannah how to plot a graph to help the three-handed man find his gloves.

"Old Millie Murdoch still there then?" Eve grinned. "Must be getting a bit long in the tooth now, I'd think. She taught me when I was at Manningham!"

"What was Millie like when she was younger?" asked Hannah curiously. It was impossible to imagine the teacher without gray hair and anxious lines around her eyes.

"Stupid old clown even then, I bet!" said Sam.

"No, she wasn't stupid," replied Eve, frowning. "Strange, but not stupid so much."

"How do you mean, strange?" asked Hannah.

"Oh, I don't know." Eve sounded vague. "It's such a long time ago, I don't really remember what all the rumors were about now." She yawned and began clearing the table.

"What rumors?" persisted Hannah, helping to stack plates.

Eve screwed up her eyes in an effort to think back. "I seem to remember one or two funny things happened in class that no one could explain at the time. Probably just us kids wanting to make some excitement in our lives!"

"What kind of funny things?"

Mrs. Fallon stood thoughtfully with a handful of knives. "I remember one thing," she said. "There were these two lads in our class. Martin Dobson and Brian . . . what was his name now?" She shook her head. "Can't recall. Anyhow, these two were always giving Millie the runaround. Calling out and saying things to make the other kids laugh and generally making her life difficult. Trouble was, they were good at their sums, better than the rest of us, and I reckon they got bored and acted up."

"Don't blame them," announced Sam, leaning against the wall and bouncing a tennis ball on the floor.

"Stop that," said his mother.

"Go on, please, Mrs. Fallon," said Hannah.

"Yes, well, one day I remember these two were being extra-specially obstreperous like, and Millie set down her chalk and gave them such a look!"

"What kind of look?"

Eve screwed up her eyes again. "Kind of a long, hard stare. We all saw it, though we didn't take too much notice at the time. Anyway, the next day, neither of those boys turned up for school."

"Just goofing off," said Sam scornfully.

"And they didn't turn up the next day, neither,"

said his mother, ignoring the interruption. "Nor the one after that, nor the one after that! Then when they did come at last, it turned out they'd both woken in the middle of the night with this terrible allover rash—like chicken pox—only it wasn't chicken pox. The doctor said he'd never seen the like of it before. It left scars too. On their faces especially."

Sam had gone very quiet. He had stopped bouncing the tennis ball and was running a finger along his cheek thoughtfully.

Eve picked up a pile of plates and was about to carry them out to the kitchen when she glanced through the window. "Quick! Social worker!" she hissed urgently.

Hannah leaped up from her chair in alarm and watched, fascinated, as the whole family, including the twins, went into a rapid and apparently well-rehearsed routine. It was rather like seeing an expert scene change in the theater. The table was cleared and a sliced loaf of bread and a tub of margarine appeared instead. The TV set was wheeled behind a curtain, two shabby blankets were thrown over the new chair covers, the twins had their shoes removed and ancient, hand-knitted sweaters thrust over their heads, and Eve's canary-yellow blouse was concealed beneath a faded cotton smock.

Seconds later the doorbell rang.

"Good afternoon, Mrs. Fallon," came a mournful voice from the doorway. "I was just passing and thought I'd drop in to see how you're all getting on. I hope this isn't an inconvenient time for you?"

"Oh, no," replied Eve, demurely looking down at the carpet, which she'd just had time to cover with a couple of moth-eaten felt rugs. "But you must take us as you find us, I'm afraid. We don't get much company, only Hannah here. She's a friend of young Sam's, and we treat her like one of the family. We haven't much, but what we have we like to share, isn't that right, Sam?"

Fortunately the woman didn't see Sam's face during this heroic speech because she was too busy looking at his saintly mother. The social worker was earnest and middle-aged, with a large, pale face and round glasses resting on a wide, flat nose. She wore a plaid skirt and a pair of sensible brown shoes with laces.

"Well, I must say it all looks most neat and clean," she was saying. "Really, I don't know how you manage. I do admire the way you're coping. It must be very difficult for you."

"There's no point letting things get you down,"

said Eve bravely. "We do very well, all things considered."

Nobody could deny that, thought Hannah.

"We must see about getting you something extra for the children's clothing allowance before the winter sets in, and I expect you'll be needing some help with the electricity bill."

Eve cast down her eyes and managed a pathetic smile, then turned and winked broadly at Hannah behind the visitor's back. Hannah did her best to keep a straight face.

"Well, as I said, this is just an unofficial call, and I'll be along again on Wednesday morning as arranged."

Eve showed the social worker out and reappeared a moment later.

"Darn woman!" she exclaimed. "Why can't she give us a bit of warning instead of just popping up like a rat out of a drainpipe? What's she doing checking up on us on a Saturday, anyway? She should leave decent folk alone to enjoy their weekend!"

Hannah giggled and watched while the stage routine quickly went into reverse and the room and the twins were restored to normal. Then she looked at her watch. "I really ought to be going now, Mrs.

Fallon. Thanks very much for everything."

"You're very welcome, my love. Come again soon. Now, how are you getting home?"

"I'll walk to the city center and catch a bus from there."

"Do you want Sam to walk with you? It's getting late."

"No, it's okay, thanks. I think I might just stop at the cathedral on the way home."

Sam's eyebrows rose in disbelief. "What do you want in that old place?"

"Don't be rude, Sam. If Hannah wants to go there, it's no business of yours. Besides, I'm sure it's a very nice place if you're fond of that kind of thing. A bit drafty of course and must cost a lot to heat, and as for cleaning it! Well, all I can say is I'm glad it's not my job. Especially those great windows. Just think of the polishing!"

Hannah had no idea if the cathedral would even be open at that time on a Saturday evening; all the same, she was hoping to catch another glimpse of the Virgin and Child, just in case those calm, gentle features might shed some light on what had happened yesterday. But when she got there she found a small crowd of people gathered outside the west door and a police car parked on the gravel, its blue light flashing urgently in the darkness.

"Do you know what's happened?" she asked a man in a raincoat who was staring vacantly at the police car, his hands in his pockets.

"Not sure exactly," he replied. "Something about a missing child."

It seemed a funny place to lose a child. Feeling flat with disappointment, Hannah walked to the bus stop.

That night she dreamed that Eve Fallon was swinging high above the ground on an enormous steel platform, trying to clean the great west window with a bottle of ammonia and a very small sponge.

CHAPTER SEVEN

THE THEFT

As Hannah was finishing dressing on Sunday morning, there was a light tap on her door and she opened it to see her father standing outside, twisting his hands together in front of him and looking uneasy. "Just thought I'd remind you," he began apologetically. "It's—"

"It's okay, Dad," said Hannah. "I hadn't forgotten. It's the anniversary. October the thirtieth."

"Ah. Knew you'd remember. You always do."

"How is she?"

"Just the same as always—you know how she gets."

"Has she, um, said anything?"

"No, no." Her father shook his head. "If only she would, it would make it so much easier."

"I know. How about you, Dad? Are you all right?"

"Not too bad. It's worse for her, of course. Well, just thought I'd mention it." He turned away, closing the door quietly behind him.

Hannah sat on the edge of her bed and sighed. Exactly fourteen years since her brother Tom had been born and exactly fourteen years since he had died. And not once in all the time she could remember had her mother mentioned, or even alluded to, the fact. It was just as though the episode had never taken place and Hannah had been simply an only child, which she was, of course. But she might not have been, had things turned out differently.

Slowly she made her way downstairs and into the kitchen.

"Good morning!" Her mother's voice was aggressively cheerful. "Sleep well?"

"Not bad. What about you?"

"Like a log! Fancy a poached egg? I'm doing one for your father."

"Thanks. I'll make some toast." She took two slices of bread and put them in the toaster. Then she fetched two plates from the cupboard. "You not having anything?"

"Not just yet," replied Mom brightly. "I might have something a bit later on."

The toast was slightly burned and brittle, and as Hannah tried to spread butter on it, it broke up, as if it had already taken on the fragile atmosphere in the room. She felt a spasm of irritation. Why did Mom have to be like this? Why did she have to keep herself so horribly brave all the time? It wasn't fair for any of them. Then she saw that the brightness in her mother's eyes was caused by unshed tears, and her heart contracted with pity. She longed to put her arms around her, to comfort her, but knew instinctively that it would be the wrong thing to do just then. One day maybe, but not yet. Everyone had to find their own way of coping with grief—that was what Granny said. This was her mother's way.

Breakfast was eaten in an uneasy silence, interrupted by guarded, meaningless remarks from Hannah and her father and occasional bursts of feverish chatter from Mom. When they had finished, Hannah stacked the dishwasher and escaped to her bedroom in relief.

The first thing she did was to go to her bookcase and reach behind the books on the bottom shelf, taking out a bulging, battered folder made of light-green cardboard that had once been stiff but was now limp and furry at the edges. She sat on the bed and took out a sheaf of drawings. The top ones were on real art paper, but farther back they were on ordinary plain paper and farther back still on the thick, colored construction paper she had used as a very young child. All together there were forty-eight sheets.

She looked at the top sketch, which was of a slim boy in his early teens with light-brown hair, dressed in jeans and a T-shirt and standing astride a bicycle, his hands on the handlebars and his gaze fixed on a point in the middle distance. Behind him was a field with horses in it, and to the right of the picture, in the direction of the boy's gaze, was a rocky, curving coastline, and beyond that, the sea.

Hannah smiled at the boy. He couldn't smile back because he wasn't looking at her, but she didn't mind.

Then, one by one, she went through the other drawings. There he was seated at the computer, playing a complicated-looking game; there he was again, swimming in the sea, battling against the surf on the north Cornish coast. Here he was reading a book, his chin propped on his hand in an attitude of contented absorption, and here he was again in his new high school uniform. As she went farther back he got younger, of course, and the sketching less assured. He was pictured playing ball with his father, picking strawberries with Hannah, going to the supermarket with Mom.

At the very bottom of the pile was a tattered, grubby scrap of blue construction paper. A figure with a round body, sticks for arms and legs, and huge pink ears grinned back at her from a mouth that seemed to have more than its fair share of teeth. She smiled at it. She had been four years old when she drew that, just after Granny had told her about Tom. She remembered the fascination she had felt at knowing she so nearly had a big brother. Her infant imagination pictured him at the age of six, already tall and strong and bold. Then she drew him, confident and at ease with a pencil even at that age, and as soon as she had drawn him he was real. It was as simple as that.

Since then she had drawn him many times, at each stage in his life, or rather in the life he might have had. When she was younger she used to talk to him, tell him secrets. She soon discovered that with this big brother she need never feel lonely because he was always there for her. Now that she was older she didn't often speak to him directly, but the sense of companionship, of sharing in the experience of growing up, remained.

No one knew about the pictures except herself. It wasn't that they were secret exactly, just private. There were times when she would have liked to tell Mom, and show her the fine son he was growing into, but she was afraid that her mother might be angry, or worse, made even more unhappy by the forty-eight reminders of what might have been.

She replaced the drawings, closed the folder, and put it back behind the shelf. Then she unenthusiastically took out her science book and tried to concentrate on writing up an experiment on energy and conduction they had done in class at the beginning of the week. It had involved three rods, of copper, iron, and glass, each with a thumbtack fixed to the end. They had then heated the ends of the rods equally with a bunsen burner and recorded the time taken for each of the thumbtacks to fall off. Part of the reason for the experiment was to see which of the three materials would be most suitable for making a saucepan.

Hannah sighed and started to draw the diagram. She wasn't especially interested in the experiment itself, but she always enjoyed diagrams and knew that they would help her grade even if she didn't get the writing up of the experiment quite right.

Then a sentence in her textbook caught her eye.

"In energy transfers, the energy spreads out to more and more places. As it spreads, it becomes less useful to us."

Her mind wandered away from bunsen burners and saucepans, back to last Friday afternoon in the cold cathedral. The chill had struck her the moment she'd stood on the enormous mat. But then as soon as she'd started to draw the statues she had felt warm. More than warm. Hot. So hot in fact that when she had finished, she felt faint and had to put her head down. And what had that chaplain said? "Strange place to faint—it certainly can't be the heat. Seems even colder in here than usual!"

Heat was energy, she knew that. Hannah pushed the book aside and put her head in her hands, thinking hard. If energy became less useful when it spread out, it was logical to assume that it would be more useful when it was all in one place. Supposing that for those few moments when she drew the Virgin and Child, all the energy in the vast building had focused on her?

She shook herself impatiently. She must be going crazy to be spooked by a school textbook!

A smell of cooking wafted into the room, and she went downstairs to set the table for lunch. Nobody was hungry, but Hannah and her father made a brave effort to cope with the roast leg of lamb her mother had insisted on cooking, just as if this were a Sunday no different from any other.

When the meal was over and cleared away, she left her parents sitting over coffee and went outside for a breath of fresh air. Mom seemed slightly calmer now, but she thought they probably needed to be by themselves for a while. Besides, the atmosphere in the house felt saturated with a sadness that seemed to weigh everything down, like a blanket left on the clothesline in the rain.

The afternoon was sullen and overcast, with the dull, windless lethargy of a day that had seen no glimpse of sun and wasn't ever likely to now. She turned left out of the front door and walked briskly away from the direction of the main road, along half a dozen streets all very much like her own, to a little park where two small children were playing on the swings. They were watched by a young man who stood looking awkward and bored, his hands in his pockets, waiting for the time when he could reasonably take the children home, his duty discharged for another week.

Hannah sat down on a bench whose back was covered in graffiti and watched the two children playing. The girl was about six, and the boy, presumably her brother, two or three years older. They began to squabble aimlessly, while their father stood helpless and impatient. The age gap was about the same as the one between herself and Tom, she thought. Would they have been like that, quarrelsome and competitive, and would Dad have looked bored and irritated when he took them to play in the park on a Sunday afternoon?

She had a sudden urge to run up to the little family and shake each of them in turn—to tell the girl how lucky she was to have a big brother, the father how fortunate to have two children and not just one. But that was ridiculous. For all she knew he wasn't their father at all. Or maybe he was and their mother had died, or left home, and the three of them were feeling miserable and grief stricken. She would never know. You never really did know about other people.

Her parents were watching television when she got home, or rather Dad was dozing, the newspaper strewn chaotically around him and his glasses upside down on the arm of the chair, while Mom watched an old film at the same time as trying to restore order to the pages. Toby lay on his side on the hearthrug, tabby fur disheveled, legs straight and mouth slightly open, looking as usual like the victim of a hit-and-run driver until Hannah nudged him with her foot and he twitched his tail, opening one eye in mild protest. She curled up in an armchair to watch the rest of the film, but soon lost interest as the warmth of the room after the fresh air made her sleepy.

At six o'clock she was roused by the busy, important-sounding music that introduced the news, and she went into the kitchen to get something to drink. But when she came back her father was wide-awake and both parents were staring anxiously at the TV screen, their eyes wide with alarm and fixed on a picture of the cathedral. Their cathedral.

"Is this the regional news already?" asked Hannah.

"Shh!" Her father silenced her impatiently. "It's the national news!"

"The disappearance was noticed by a member of the cathedral staff yesterday evening," the announcer was saying. "He alerted the police immediately, but they were unable to trace the thief, or thieves, who apparently escaped unnoticed with the departing congregation."

The camera panned diagonally from the southwest corner of the building before coming to rest on the north side, just to the left of the altar.

There was the statue of the Virgin, but in the curve of her arms, where the baby should have been, was an empty space.

❖ CHAPTER EIGHT ❖

MR. CRISTANTHI

On Monday morning all the national newspapers carried the story of the stolen statue on the front page, and *The Times* devoted an article to the history of the wooden figures, mentioning the fact that they were among the very few religious images not destroyed during the sixteenth-century dissolution of the monasteries.

Hannah had slept badly and woken early. For once she couldn't face anything to eat, but she grabbed an apple from the fruit bowl. She wasn't able to wear her coat because she had lent it to Katie on Friday afternoon, but for some reason she couldn't find her scarf either. She took a jacket from the peg in the hall and set off for the bus stop.

It was while she was on the bus that she realized

she had last had her scarf in the cathedral. She remembered taking it off because she was too hot, but couldn't remember putting it on before she left. It was unlikely that anyone would be interested in looking for her scarf when there was something a lot more important to find, but there was just a chance that it had been picked up and put somewhere, or perhaps there was a lost and found. It was worth a try.

When she reached the cathedral square, the place was already lively with inquisitive sightseers, camera-laden reporters, and busy-looking policemen. Although a sign said CATHEDRAL CLOSED TODAY, the main door was open and Hannah walked quickly up the gravel path and slipped inside as inconspicuously as possible, before anyone had a chance to turn her away.

Half a dozen people were grouped around the statue, talking in low voices or taking photographs—something that now seemed to be allowed—but none of them took any notice of her. Another group of people was photographing a patch of wall to the right of the west door, and two more were bent almost double, apparently searching the floor for something small.

"Can I help you?"

She recognized the day chaplain with relief. "Oh! Do you remember, I came in on Friday and I spoke to you? I think I must have left my scarf here then. Has anyone found it?"

The man looked harassed. "I'm afraid not. Not as far as I know. A lot of things seem to have gone missing lately." His voice was grim.

"Of course! I'm so sorry. About the statue I mean." As soon as the words were out of her mouth she thought how painfully inadequate they were, but she couldn't think what else to say. She glanced at the couple searching the floor. "What are they looking for?"

"Good heavens!" exclaimed the chaplain. "That's the pair who lost an earring in here yesterday. I saw them at the door and told them that they couldn't come in. The police have closed the building to the public." He looked at her severely. "Now I come to think of it, how did you get in?"

"The door was open. They must have left it like that when they came in."

Frowning, he strode toward the couple who were still staring at the floor, and Hannah was about to leave when she caught sight of the statue of the Virgin, and her heart gave an unexpected lurch.

Something about the face had changed. It was still smiling, but it was as if a shadow fell across the eyes, and the soft, gentle mouth showed pain. Pain and something else. Pride. Pride to bear pain. Hannah had seen that look before. It was the look her mother had worn yesterday while she was fiercely poaching eggs in the kitchen.

Tears filled her eyes and threatened to spill over. She felt in her pocket for a tissue and hurriedly pulled one out. With it came a quantity of small coins that rolled in all directions over the stone floor. Several heads turned to stare, and she bent down, blushing with embarrassment. One of the coins had rolled behind a pillar that was very close to the cathedral wall. Hannah reached her hand in as far as it would go and her fingers found the coin. Withdrawing it, she discovered that it was attached to a large ball of fluff with various other small objects in tow. While she was examining them, the chaplain approached.

Hastily, Hannah bundled the coins and assorted oddments into her tissue, stuffed it in her pocket, and made her way to the rear of the building.

As she got near the west door, the group of photographers shifted slightly and she was able to see the patch of wall that was causing so much interest.

On it hung a small wooden crucifix. It was oddly misshapen. Then she saw why. Someone had hung it upside down.

When she got to school, the first thing she did was to put her math homework—the completed graph— in Miss Murdoch's pigeonhole near the staff room. As she turned to go back to the classroom she noticed a young man standing near the water fountain. He looked vaguely familiar, but she couldn't think where she might have seen him before. He gave her a friendly smile and she smiled back, wondering who he was. Visitors usually had a plastic-covered tag with their name on to show they hadn't just wandered in off the street, but this man had no tag, though he didn't look like an intruder.

In the classroom everyone seemed to be talking about last night's TV news. Nothing so exciting had happened in the city for as long as any of them could remember, and they were going to make the most of it before they had to settle down for a history lesson.

"My dad thinks it was kids who did it," said Jason.

"That's nice!" retorted Susie. "Why pick on the young and innocent?"

"I think it was some weird religious cult," said

Rani. "You know, the kind of people who get together in a big, old house somewhere and end up killing each other!"

"You've been watching too many horror movies," said Sam.

They were still discussing the theft when Mr. Nuffield, the vice principal, walked in accompanied by the man Hannah had seen outside the staff room. The chatter stopped abruptly, and 8B watched expectantly as the two men walked to the front of the classroom and Mr. Nuffield turned to address them.

He began by clearing his throat rather self-consciously.

"Unfortunately, we heard last night that Mrs. Crawford has been taken ill and has had to go to the hospital," he told them in the voice of a news-caster who has serious news to impart but wants to make it clear it's not all bad. "However!" Now he glanced around cheerfully. "We are very lucky that Mr. Cristanthi is able to step in at short notice, to take her place until she gets better."

He beamed at them all and Hannah wondered if they were expected to applaud. Instead they shuffled uneasily and Mr. Nuffield looked embarrassed, as if he'd lost his place.

"Well," he finished up, "I'll, um, leave you to it!" And off he went, leaving the new teacher to face the class.

"Good morning!" Mr. Cristanthi's voice was clear and confident, his manner enthusiastic; a ripple of interest ran through the class. He was not especially tall, but slim and muscular, with close-cropped dark hair, olive skin, a full mouth, and a short, very straight nose. His dark-brown eyes looked as if they could be thrilling or unnerving depending on whether or not you'd done your homework. Right away, he held their attention.

"I understand that you are currently studying the causes and effects of the Second World War?" He waited for a few seconds for a murmur of assent before continuing. "In that case, I would like to tell you something of what went on in London during the Blitz."

He began to tell the class of wailing air-raid sirens, screaming German bombers, toppling buildings, unquenchable fires, and the eerie, suffocating darkness of the blackout. He told them of a family's miraculous escape from a burning terraced house, with the other houses in the terrace collapsing all around them. They could smell the smoke, hear the screams, feel the intense heat, see the leaping, hungry tongues of flame.

After twenty-five minutes he recalled them to the present day and they all breathed freely and unclenched their hands, then looked around sheepishly at one another, embarrassed at getting so worked up and involved in a history lesson.

"Now I wonder how many of you know of the damage inflicted on this city. It was not only London that was bombed, you know."

"My grandmother can remember when Dylan's store was just a pile of smoking rubble!" announced Sophie proudly.

"And my uncle says the reason why the shopping district in front of the cathedral was built was because all the old shops were destroyed in the bombing raids!" This came from Rani, whose parents ran the Indian restaurant on the edge of the district.

"The Empire cinema had its box office blown up right in the middle of a newsreel about British troops!" called out Jason.

Everyone was eager to contribute something, eager to impress the new teacher.

"But the cathedral wasn't damaged, was it?" murmured Emily, her beautiful eyes showing deep feeling and respect.

"No," Mr. Cristanthi said with a smile. "The

cathedral, it seems, enjoyed divine protection! Now I think we have plenty of information here. I would like to suggest that we begin a project, with each of you choosing one building from this city that interests you and that survived the bombs. You should write a report about the history of the building, and it should have plenty of illustrations in the form of either drawings or photographs, and perhaps some newspaper clippings if you can get hold of them. You will have plenty of time to complete the project—it can be handed in at the end of the semester."

After he had gone, the class buzzed with excitement.

"He's gorgeous!" exclaimed Susie.

"Cool," murmured Sophie.

"Wicked!" said Rani.

Everyone agreed on one thing, however: Mr. Cristanthi was a brilliant teacher, and although none of them wished Mrs. Crawford any particular harm, no one was in any hurry for her to get better too soon.

Hannah and Sam sat together at lunchtime, discussing the theft. Hannah still hadn't mentioned the sketch to anyone except her father, and although she really wanted to tell Sam, she didn't feel quite ready for the cold blast of common sense that she knew would follow.

"Why would anybody want to steal a little wooden statue?" Hannah's forehead was furrowed and her mouth full of spaghetti hoops. "I know it's valuable, but you couldn't sell it, could you? Especially not if it was separated from the other part?"

"No!" Sam's voice was derisive. "You could never sell a thing like that! Too well-known. It'd be like trying to flog the *Moaning Lisa*."

"*Mona Lisa*, you dope. So why? Do you think it was just a joke, and eventually they'll put it back?"

"Maybe." He shrugged. "There's some people who just like trashing things for the sake of it."

"Like vandals, you mean?" This was a terrible thought. Had somebody taken an axe to the tiny figure?

"Kind of, but not just stupid people. I mean, take computers. You need to be really smart to create a computer virus, and the people who do it could probably make a load in computers anyway, but instead they get a thrill out of making chaos for some poor user, or, if they're really good at it, for some multinational company."

"You mean they can see that something's good,

and working well, and they just want to destroy it?"

"I suppose so. Don't know any hackers, but they'd have to be seriously sick to do what they do."

At that moment Susie appeared at their table. "Hi, Hannah! Did you do the masks?"

Hannah looked bewildered. "What masks?"

"The Halloween masks of course! You said you'd do one each for you, me, and Sam, so we could go trick-or-treating this evening!"

Hannah put her hand up to her mouth in dismay. The theft of the statue had put all thoughts of Halloween out of her mind.

"Sorry, Susie," she said. "I completely forgot." She looked at her watch. "I've just got time to get some cardboard from the art room and I'll do them after school."

"Thanks! See you later."

As soon as the afternoon's lessons were over, Hannah took two pieces of black cardboard from her desk with some felt-tipped pens, and set to work. Susie and Sam, as well as one or two others, gathered around to watch. Hannah's quick, accurate drawing fascinated them and soon several people were asking for masks of their own.

"I've only got enough cardboard for two," she

said, feeling slightly relieved. She could see herself busy for the next hour or so, making masks for the entire class.

She swiftly drew Susie a witch, complete with pointed hat, long, straggly hair, and a particularly repulsive warty nose.

"Wow!" said Susie, when holes had been cut for the eyes and mouth. She held it up to her face and the others shrieked in mock horror.

Sam, at his own request, was a vampire, with long canines realistically dripping blood, narrow slits for eyes, and a wicked leer.

"I can't see," he complained, trying it on for size.

"If I cut the eyes any bigger you'll look kind and trustworthy," she told him.

He willingly accepted the risk of breaking his neck in return for looking thoroughly evil.

"You'll have to put some elastic on when you get home." Hannah got up and started to pack her book bag before leaving.

"What about you? You haven't done your own mask," said Susie.

"I know. If you don't mind, I think I won't come tonight. I'm kind of tired." For some reason the last thing she felt like doing was celebrating Halloween.

"Oh, come on! You'll stop being tired as soon as we get going."

"Yeah. Don't be such a wimp," said Sam as they walked down the corridor. Every so often he lunged at the people they passed, and they screamed cheerfully at the dripping fangs.

"Please, Hannah," said Susie. "It's no fun with only two, and you did promise." She looked disappointed.

"I haven't got a coat to wear. Katie Brown borrowed mine and she wasn't in school today."

"Wear something else then!"

"I've got homework to finish."

"We don't have to be out for long."

"And it's too late to do a mask now."

"That's no problem," said Sam. "Your mom's bound to have an old sheet or something. You can come as a ghost!"

"Oh, all right."

CHAPTER NINE

HALLOWEEN

Never had a more reluctant ghost set off trick-or-treating at Halloween. Fortunately, Sam and Susie were having too much fun to notice that Hannah was less than enthusiastic and they pranced along, practicing bloodcurdling screams that made the pigeons take flight in alarm.

The first house they visited brought them down to earth a bit when the owner, a burly man with tattoos on his arms, told them to get lost before he called the police, and the next five doors they knocked at remained firmly shut. Either the owners were out for the evening or they had decided not to entertain trick-or-treaters.

"Let's try a different neighborhood," suggested Sam. "This one's dead."

They walked for a while in the direction of the city center until they came to a street where most of the houses were brightly lit and there were other people wearing Halloween costumes. Here they had more success. The residents were suitably impressed with the masks and generous with their treats.

Munching contentedly, Sam and Susie turned left at a street corner with Hannah following at a mutinous distance. Suddenly she noticed the name on the street sign.

"Hey!" she called. "This is Martindale Road. That's where Millie Murdoch lives! I know because I'm supposed to go there for extra math tutoring this week."

"What number?" asked Sam.

"Eighty-two, I think. Or was it eighty-three? No, eighty-two."

"Cool!" Sam smiled wickedly behind his mask. "Come on! Let's go and give Mad Millie the fright of her life!"

But when the door of number eighty-two opened, it was Sam, Susie, and Hannah who had a fright.

Miss Murdoch was standing in a darkened hallway, wearing a long purple robe with a hem embroidered with stars and moons, a heavy chain around her neck, and enormous gold hoops in her ears. Her gray hair was loose on her shoulders and she held a tall white candle in a brass candlestick. Beyond her in the gloom, they could dimly make out an open door that shed a pallid light on a round dining table where a collection of people all dressed as strangely as herself were sitting, apparently eating a meal in complete silence.

"Who goes there on the great Feast of Samhain?" intoned Miss Murdoch sepulchrally.

"On the what?" asked Sam in a voice quite unlike a vampire's.

"The Day of the Dead! The Great Blood Harvest!"

Hannah and Susie gulped, but Sam wasn't going to be intimidated by Mad Millie, even if she was wearing a fancy dress and talking gibberish.

"Trick-or-treat!" he said boldly.

"Wait!" Miss Murdoch raised her hand dramatically. She disappeared into a room at the back and reappeared a few moments later with a bag of re-assuringly normal-looking candy bars that she thrust into Sam's hand.

"Take your leave with care!" she whispered. "And remember, on this night the veil between the worlds is at its thinnest!"

"Thanks," muttered Sam faintly, echoed by his two companions. The door closed and the three moved away.

"Wow!" said Susie, awestruck. "I always thought she was crazy, but not that crazy!"

"She's nuts!" announced Sam, tearing open the bag of candy bars and offering them around.

Hannah was silent. Millie's talk about the Day of the Dead and the veil between the worlds had unnerved her, and in any case she felt guilty about letting the others know where she lived. It didn't seem right to let them make fun of her, especially when she'd offered to give her extra tutoring. She followed listlessly while Sam and Susie capered in front, entertaining each other with imitations of Miss Murdoch's portentous tones. A light drizzle started to fall.

"I've had enough," she told them when at last she managed to get their attention. "I think I'll go home now."

"But we've only just started!" protested Sam.

"If I go any farther I won't be able to get back on my own. This way you can see Susie home and get back yourself without having to go all the way to my house first."

Sam shrugged. "Okay. If you're sure you're all

right walking home alone."

"I'll be fine. It's only half a mile and there are tons of people about. See you tomorrow." She gave a ghostly wave to the witch and the vampire, and the witch and the vampire waved back. Then she took off the sheet, wrapped it around her neck like a scarf, and set off.

At first she walked fast, turning over the events of the last few days in her mind and paying no attention to where she was going nor to the little groups of laughing, chattering ghouls and witches who mostly took no notice of her either. After about fifteen minutes she looked up and saw a store she didn't recognize. That was odd. She didn't remember any stores around here, only houses. She walked a bit farther, then stopped, confused. By now she should have reached the little park near her house, but there was no sign of it. Only another row of stores, all equally unfamiliar.

Then she realized. She must have taken a wrong turn without knowing and been walking for some time, not toward home but closer and closer to the center of the city. That meant that she now had twice as far to go as when she'd left Sam and Susie!

She felt in her pocket and found her bus pass.

There were plenty of buses from the city center. The best thing would be to walk farther in now and catch the bus she normally took from school.

She continued walking, hoping to see somewhere she recognized and making for the busy, brightly lit streets. Now quite a lot of people were out, spilling from pubs and restaurants. She peered at a street sign, and a man wearing a long red cloak with a pair of flashing horns on his head sprang out at her from a doorway. As she jumped to avoid him she fell against a creature with a blood-streaked, corpselike mask on its face.

"Here! Watch where you're going!" said the corpse angrily, and two girls wearing incongruously short skirts with tall pointed hats laughed shrilly.

Hannah started to feel scared. Why hadn't she stayed with the others?

"Excuse me." She stopped a man wearing a black T-shirt with skeleton ribs on it. "Can you tell me where I can get the seventy-one bus?"

The man stared at her in mock horror. "Help! A monster!" he cried, to shouts of mirth from his friends.

Then to her relief, she saw the great mass of the cathedral looming in the distance and the sign of the Black Bear Inn on the corner of St. Peter's

Street, and she realized where she was. But the bus stop was on the other side of the cathedral square, which was now so thronged with noisy revelers that it would take half an hour at least to cross it.

The Black Bear had a crowd of drinkers on the sidewalk outside and she knew that to reach the cathedral, she would have to find a way past them. Her heart sank. Then she saw a little alleyway at one side of the inn and she guessed that it would lead somehow to the cathedral courtyard.

The passage was narrow and dark, but at least it was empty of drunken merrymakers and Hannah followed it down the side of the building till she reached a little cobbled courtyard surrounded by tall, half-timbered houses with upstairs rooms jutting out over the street. This was the oldest part of the city and the houses leaned at odd angles, propping one another up like bent, decrepit old men.

The strange thing was the silence. The alleyway couldn't have been more than fifty yards long, yet the noise from the city had faded entirely. There were still a few people about, and some wore dark cloaks with hoods pulled forward to half cover their mouths, but there were no pointed hats to be seen, and no chatter or laughter. On the doors of two of the houses someone had scrawled black crosses, and a wooden cart leaned against a wall. There was a strange smell. Like roasting meat, but more pungent and sickly. It filled her head and made her dizzy.

The opposite side of the courtyard should, she thought, lead to Tanner's Lane, and at the end of Tanner's Lane was the bus stop. But although she strained her eyes, she could see no opening between the houses.

She began to feel uneasy. Why was it so quiet here? Suddenly she wanted to be back in the noise and chaos of the cathedral square, but to get there, she had to go back the way she had come. She turned back toward the alleyway, her eyes searching for the brightly lit street at the end, but she couldn't see that far as the path seemed to bend at a slight angle. She forced herself into the dark, narrow passage again and ran down it a little distance until she knew she must be more than halfway. Then she stopped. There was no light at the end of the passage. No light, and no noise.

She tried to reason with herself. Maybe she had become disoriented and that was the wrong alleyway. If so, the entrance to the other one must be close by. She looked around for somebody to ask, but the few people she had seen earlier now seemed to have disappeared. The silence hung heavily and she was no longer merely uneasy; she was beginning to be afraid. Her heart beat uncomfortably fast as she crossed the greasy cobbles in search of an opening between the houses, and as she did so, an old man came forward out of the shadows.

The man wore a ragged brown cloak, and his feet were bound in strips of rotting cloth, to which clung shreds of sawdust. He walked slowly toward her, then stopped and pointed in the direction of her right hip. Then he looked at her, and Hannah saw, even in the gloom, that his eyes were bright blue.

She stared down and realized that he was pointing at her pocket. Trembling with a mixture of fear and relief that the man was just a beggar, she reached in, pulled out a coin, and offered it to him. But the man only looked at it in puzzlement and shook his head. Then he pointed to her pocket again.

"But that's all I have!" Her voice sounded tinny, unresonant.

Still the old man continued to point, and at last she was forced to draw out the only other thing she had, which was a balled-up tissue.

To her utter astonishment, the old man took the tissue, unfolded it, and stared at it for a long time.

Then he spoke, and at first Hannah thought he must be foreign, so strange did the words sound. Like a key turning slowly in a rusty lock. But as she listened, she realized that he seemed to be speaking English, though with such a strong dialect that she could hardly make it out. He seemed to say, "'Tis bitook to thee, be rayit not."

But before she could ask him what he meant, he carefully folded the tissue and handed it back to her. Then he stepped back into the shadow of a doorway and seemed to disappear into the darkness.

The noise of a distant police car broke the silence, and after a few moments she realized that she could hear voices and the sounds of traffic. As little groups of people appeared, she saw that the black cloaks were only dark raincoats with hoods, the crosses on the doors were sprayed on with graffiti paint, and the smell of roasting meat came from a hamburger stand set up against the courtyard wall.

Now she found that she could see clearly ahead of her another, opposite alleyway that led out toward the cathedral. She must have missed it in the darkness. Slowly she followed it to the end, turned right, and walked down Tanner's Lane to the bus stop, where a number seventy-one was just pulling in.

The bus was crowded and noisy, but she managed to find a seat near the back and sat down heavily, suddenly drained and exhausted.

She pulled the tissue out of her pocket and looked again at the dusty collection of small objects she had picked up from the cathedral floor. A paper clip, a rubber band, a candy-bar wrapper, a bit of stick, and a coin. That was all. Nothing of any value to anyone.

So what had the old man been trying to tell her? She repeated the strange words over and over in her head, as if by doing so the rusty lock and key might turn and give up their secret, but it was no use. Probably he was just crazy, or drunk, and had scared her because he'd appeared so suddenly out of the darkness when her nerves were already on edge. And the silence, the darkness? That was easily explained by the fact that the little courtyard was effectively cut off from the main square by the height and closeness of the old houses. She must have imagined the rest. Otherwise, what could have happened?

The alternative was too frightening to consider. She couldn't go there.

Nevertheless, when she was in bed later that night, she took a piece of paper and wrote down the words of the old man, exactly as she had heard them.

She stared at what she had written. "'Tis bitook to thee, be rayit not." The words looked like writing remembered from a dream: charged with significance at the time, but in the end quite meaningless.

At last she turned off the light, but it was a long time before she fell into a fitful, exhausted sleep.

CHAPTER TEN

INTERVIEW WITH THE POLICE

The first thing she noticed when she got to school the next day was that her coat had been returned. That was a relief, as in the last few days the weather had turned cold.

As soon as the class attendance was taken, Miss Rycroft, 8B's homeroom teacher, came over to Hannah's desk. "Mr. Andrade wants to see you in his office," she said.

"What, now?"

"Yes, now," replied the teacher firmly.

"Did he say what about?"

Miss Rycroft shook her head but looked worried, and Hannah felt uneasy. She was rarely called to the principal's office.

When she got there, she saw that he wasn't alone. With him was a man with gray hair and a thin mustache.

"Come in, Hannah," said the principal. "There's nothing to be alarmed about."

Up until then Hannah had been more puzzled than alarmed, but as soon as Mr. Andrade said that, she felt a twinge of worry. If there was nothing to be alarmed about, then why mention it?

"This is Detective Sergeant Bean, and he would like to have a word with you." Mr. Andrade smiled at Hannah but didn't get up, so she assumed that he was going to stay.

"Now, Miss Price," began Sergeant Bean formally, "I'll come straight to the point. I'm sure I don't have to tell you that last Saturday afternoon a very valuable piece of property was removed from the cathedral."

"Yes," replied Hannah. "I mean . . . no."

"You mean you didn't know?"

"I mean you didn't have to tell me."

Sergeant Bean frowned. He hoped it wasn't going to be a difficult interview.

"Anyhow," he continued, "we've been talking to members of the cathedral staff, trying to find out if they remembered anyone acting sus . . . that is . . .

um, unusually, at any time before the incident took place."

He looked at Hannah, but she said nothing. She was beginning to feel distinctly uncomfortable.

"The thing is, Miss Price," went on the sergeant, "that one of those day chaplains said he noticed a young lady taking a close interest in this piece of property only the previous day."

"Me, you mean." Her mouth had suddenly gone dry.

"He says you made a drawing of the statues. A very good one, I believe."

"Did you, Hannah?" asked Mr. Andrade.

She nodded.

"And that afterward, you seemed . . . distracted. Maybe even a bit"—he looked down at his notes— "'obsessed' was the word he used, I believe."

"I see. You think I stole the statue." She felt as if she were in a nightmare and would wake up soon.

"You're not being accused of anything, Hannah," interrupted Mr. Andrade. "Right?" He turned to the policeman anxiously.

"Of course not," said Sergeant Bean hastily. "We just want to follow up on anything that happened leading to the disappearance of the statue. Now." He leaned forward. "Why don't you start by telling me why you decided to draw those figures on Friday afternoon?"

"I didn't . . . decide to," said Hannah slowly. "There was a thunderstorm, you see, and I didn't have a coat. I went into the cathedral to get out of the rain."

"And then you immediately sat down and made a detailed sketch of the Virgin and Child?"

"Yes."

"Can you tell us why?" The policeman's voice was kind, and Hannah bit her lip, which was beginning to tremble.

"Why did you draw the statues?" he repeated.

"I . . . don't know," she whispered. "I liked them."

"And afterward? Were you . . . upset by anything?"

"I felt faint. Hot."

"Yet I believe," here Sergeant Bean consulted his notes again, "that the temperature was particularly cold in the cathedral that day."

"Surely it's possible that she was ill!" protested Mr. Andrade.

"And were you? Ill?" persisted the policeman gently.

"I don't know."

"Well, now," said Sergeant Bean, sitting up

straight again. "Tell us what you were up to on Saturday afternoon."

Relief flooded through her. "I was at the cinema with Sam Fallon."

"And what time did you leave?"

"I'm not sure. About four o'clock, I think."

"And then?"

"We went back to his mom's apartment."

"And she is . . . ?"

"Mrs. Fallon."

There was a short pause. Hannah looked up and saw that Mr. Andrade was looking worried.

"Would that be . . . Mrs. Arthur Fallon, by any chance?" asked the policeman.

"Sam's dad is called Arthur, yes."

"The same Arthur Fallon who is at present serving a sentence for housebreaking?" The tone was mild, but the implications didn't escape Hannah.

"But . . . you don't think . . . I . . . they . . . ?" She started to panic.

"I don't think anything, Miss Price, except that I have to confess to being a little, shall we say, surprised at the company you keep."

"Sam's not a criminal!" she said angrily. "And neither's his mother!"

The sergeant raised his eyebrows but didn't reply

to this. "Was anyone else there? Apart from the Fallons?"

"No. Yes! The social worker! I forgot about her! She visited Mrs. Fallon that afternoon. She'll remember me!"

The policeman relaxed visibly. "Ah. Now we're getting somewhere. I don't suppose you can remember her name?"

Hannah shook her head.

"Never mind, there's bound to be a record of the visit. We can check it this afternoon. What time did she arrive?"

"About five, I should think. Maybe a bit later."

"And she stayed, how long?"

"I'm not sure. Ten minutes. Fifteen at the most."

The sergeant narrowed his eyes very slightly and pursed his lips thoughtfully. Then he smiled at her. "I see. Well, that all seems quite straightforward. I'm sorry to have troubled you both, but we do have to check every possible lead, you understand. Now there's just one more thing." He reached beneath the desk and withdrew a clear plastic bag, which he handed to her. Inside was her school scarf, neatly folded.

"But the chaplain said he couldn't find it!"

Hannah felt irrationally hurt.

"I believe he discovered it shortly after you reported it missing," replied the policeman. "It has the school crest on it and your name taped to the corner. That was how we were able to trace you."

He stood up, and Mr. Andrade stood up with him. Sergeant Bean shook hands with Hannah, and the two men left the room.

She stayed where she was for a few moments, then got up and walked slowly back to her classroom.

At break time she went into the library. She took her book bag with her so it would look as if she had work to do, but the truth was that she needed to be by herself for a while. She found an empty bay, sat down, and after a few moments took out the sketch she had made in the cathedral and laid it on the table in front of her.

"Why did you draw the statues?" That was what the sergeant had asked her. When she hadn't answered, he'd asked her again.

She remembered the day chaplain. "That's remarkable! . . . You're quite an artist, young lady!" He had seemed such a nice man. But he'd been the one to tell the police about her. Did he think she could have stolen the baby?

The strain of the interview and the strangeness of the last few days suddenly overwhelmed her, and tears rolled slowly down her cheeks, falling onto the paper with light taps.

"Hannah? Hannah!"

She looked up to see Emily Rhodes standing at her shoulder.

"What's the matter?"

"Nothing," muttered Hannah, wiping her eyes with the back of her hand. "I'm okay." She didn't think she could bear Emily's kindness just at that moment.

"Well, this drawing's not okay. You've made it all wet!" Emily sat down beside her and peered at the damp sheet of paper on the table. "Can I see?"

Hannah shrugged and raised her elbows an inch so that Emily could withdraw the sketch.

"When did you do it?"

"Friday afternoon."

Emily's eyes widened. She stared at the picture for some minutes. "It's beautiful," she said at last, in an odd, flat voice. "Is that why you're crying? Because it's been stolen?"

"No. I don't know. " She just wanted Emily to go away and leave her alone.

"Is it because of that policeman?"

"How did you know about him?" Hannah stopped crying and looked at the other girl in alarm.

"I heard Miss Rycroft say you were wanted in the office. Then later, I saw Mr. Andrade show someone to a car parked in the visitor's spot. It was a police car."

"So I guess everyone knows now."

"Not necessarily. I don't think the others noticed."

Hannah looked at her, then looked away again, bleakly. "It doesn't matter anyway," she muttered. "He just wanted to know why I—"

"Why you what?"

"Why I drew the statues. Then. The day before they were stolen."

"And what did you tell him?"

"I told him I didn't know. I don't even remember drawing them. Not really."

Emily frowned. "You mean you kind of blacked out?"

"Yes. No. Not exactly."

"You're looking very tired, Hannah. Are you overworking, maybe?"

"I'm all right. I didn't sleep well last night."

"It's just that short-term memory loss can be a sign of stress, you know. Is something worrying you? Perhaps you should see a doctor."

"Look, I'm okay. Perfectly okay." Tears welled up again, and she brushed them away angrily. If only Emily would stop being sympathetic and leave her alone! But after all, she was only trying to help. She should be grateful that someone at least was prepared to try to make sense of what had happened last Friday, and for all she knew, Emily's explanation might be the right one. Was she stressed? Well, now, certainly. But before? Friday hadn't been a good day, but she'd had other bad days without losing her memory.

"Come on," said Emily, as the bell sounded for the end of break, "time to get back to work. I'll carry your bag for you."

At lunchtime Hannah found Sam in the line for the cafeteria. "Get your lunch and come and join me at that table over there in the corner," she said. "I want to talk to you without the others hearing."

He raised his eyebrows but nodded.

The table was littered with crumbs and dirty dishes, which was presumably why no one else was sitting there, but at least they had privacy.

"What's the matter with you? You on that stupid

diet again?" Sam looked suspiciously at Hannah's tray, which held a bowl of tomato soup and an apple.

She shook her head. "Just not hungry."

"But you're always hungry!" he objected.

"Well today I'm not! Okay?"

"All right, all right. Calm down. Only wondered. What's the big secret?" He put his plate on the table and leaned behind him to throw the tray in the general direction of the caterers' cart before turning back.

"A policeman was here this morning."

Sam blew on a forkful of shepherd's pie to cool it. "Probably about someone skipping school."

"He came to see me."

The fork came to an abrupt halt within an inch of Sam's mouth. "He what?"

"He thinks I had something to do with stealing the statue."

Sam put the fork back on his plate and stared at her. "You're kidding!"

"Because of this." She brushed crumbs off the table and produced the drawing of the Virgin and Child.

"You did that?"

She nodded.

"I don't understand."

She told him briefly about what had happened in the cathedral. Then she told him what Detective Sergeant Bean had said.

When she had finished, he looked thoughtful for a moment. Then he grinned. "Shame you were visiting my family just when you needed an alibi!"

"That social worker should remember me, though."

"She didn't look like she'd notice much."

"There's something else."

"What?"

"Well, yesterday morning I went back to the cathedral because I'd left my scarf there, and I saw something. A crucifix. It was hanging on the wall, and it had been turned upside down."

Sam's eyes widened. "Cool! That's devil worship. Satanism! I've seen it on TV. You get it late at night," he explained, making Satanism sound like a form of indigestion.

"Listen," she persisted. "Remember Millie Murdoch last night? And what your mom said about her punishing those boys?"

"Bet Mom made that up just to stop me goofing around in class!"

"Maybe, but—"

"Look. If you're trying to say that Mad Millie

had something to do with stealing that statue, you're as crazy as she is."

Hannah smiled. Put like that, it did sound crazy. "Maybe she's running a secret coven. You know, for witches!"

"Millie Murdoch? Running a coven? She couldn't run a bath! Anyway, if she was, and had something to do with stealing that statue, why did the old bat come to the door all dressed up and talking like a loony?"

"She couldn't have known it was us. You and Susie had masks on and I had that sheet over my head."

"She could have guessed it'd be someone from Manningham. There'd have been a good chance. She's just nuts."

"But she might know something." Hannah was thoughtful again. "Oh well, I've got my math tutorial with her the day after tomorrow. I think I might just see if I can bring up the topic of witchcraft."

"Good luck!" replied Sam sarcastically.

On her way home from school, Hannah considered how best to tell her parents about the visit from the policeman. It was too much to hope that they wouldn't find out, but she wanted the chance to explain herself before they heard it in an official letter, either from the school or from the police themselves, or more likely both. What on earth were her parents going to say when they found out their daughter had been suspected of the theft of a priceless work of art?

But as she approached the house, her heart sank. A police car was already parked outside, and Sergeant Bean was standing on the doorstep, apparently saying good-bye. He didn't notice her as he hurried down the path, got into the car, and drove off.

When she got in, her parents were in the living room, talking quietly. They looked up as she put her head around the door, and for once Mom surprised her.

"Poor Hannah! What a terrible shock you must have had this morning. I told you you'd have been better off waiting in a café instead of the cathedral. Seems like I was right after all!"

Hannah smiled weakly and sat down, feeling both relieved and confused. She didn't suppose her mother had ever spoken to a policeman in her life, other than to ask for directions, yet here she was, calmly making a joke about a criminal investigation going on in her own house!

Oddly enough, it was Dad who seemed more worried. "The timing was bad luck," he said. "At least, I suppose it was bad luck."

"What do you mean?" asked his wife indignantly. "Of course it was bad luck! You aren't suggesting Hannah stole the statue in a fit of absentmindedness, I hope?"

"No, no. Anyway, you were with Sam, weren't you? And they're trying to get in touch with the woman from social services so she can vouch for you being there. They don't seem to have had much luck so far, but I expect they will." He nibbled his thumb thoughtfully.

It suddenly occurred to Hannah that at no time had either of her parents objected to her friendship with Sam. They knew about his father of course, but had never mentioned his rather regrettable occupation and had always been welcoming on the few occasions when Sam had come to the house. She thought they should have considered him a bad influence. Yet for some odd reason she had the impression that they considered him rather a good influence. She couldn't imagine why. Parents could be very unpredictable. And what her mother said next just went to prove it.

"Come on. Let's eat. If we're all going to be arrested, we'd better not be hungry!"

❖ CHAPTER ELEVEN ❖

OLD MAGIC

IF NUMBER 82 MARTINDALE ROAD was inhabited by a witch, it showed no sign from the outside. Two tubs of winter daisies stood on either side of the dark-blue front door, russet chrysanthemums bloomed in the borders, and a window box was bright with purple pansies. The sitting-room window had a plain net curtain primly covering its lower half, with lined blue velvet drawn back and secured at the sides by tasseled cords.

At six o'clock on Thursday evening, Hannah raised the latch of the white-painted wrought-iron gate, pushed it open, and walked slowly up the paved path to the front door. She lifted the brass knocker and let it fall gently, half hoping Millie would have forgotten she was supposed to be tutoring her and gone out. Her heart sank slightly as she heard footsteps approaching, and Miss Murdoch opened the door.

"Hannah! I'm so glad you remembered! And you've got your books? Good! Now come along, this way. I hope you won't mind us working in the kitchen, because I feel it's so much cozier in here. The dining-room table is bigger, of course, but the light is bad, and to be honest, it's not my favorite room."

The kitchen was small but up-to-date, and surprisingly well organized, with green china spice jars neatly arranged on a shelf above a gleaming microwave oven. A stainless-steel coffeemaker stood on the counter next to a brass jug filled with some of the dark-red chrysanthemums from the garden. On the wall was a pendulum clock with a clear, metallic tick.

Miss Murdoch poured two glasses of orange juice and produced a jar of cookies.

Apprehensively, Hannah opened her exercise book and prepared to be thoroughly confused for an hour or so. But to her surprise Miss Murdoch, when not facing a classroom full of children, became quite calm and rational, and by the time the hour was up, Hannah actually felt she had learned something.

"Thank you, Miss Murdoch. That was really helpful. I feel a lot clearer now, though I don't think I'm ever going to be a natural at math," she said regretfully.

"Never mind, my dear. If you keep working at it, you may surprise yourself."

Now was the moment to mention the statues, but she suddenly felt ridiculous. How could she possibly start a conversation about witchcraft in this neat, modern kitchen?

Slowly she stood up and began to put away her books. Then she noticed that standing near the sink was one of the green plastic boxes provided by the city for recycling. It was full of newspapers, and on the top was last Monday's *Times*, with the photo of the statue clearly visible on the front page. She leaned forward to get a closer look, and Miss Murdoch turned to see what she was peering at, which was what Hannah had intended.

"That was awful about the stolen baby, wasn't it?" She tried to sound casual.

"Yes, terrible," agreed Miss Murdoch, getting up to take the empty glasses to the sink. "Such a piece of history!"

"I don't suppose they'll catch whoever did it now."

"Probably not."

"People at school think it might have been done by a group of devil worshippers. Black magic. That kind of thing." It was not quite true, but she needed to get a reaction.

"Well now! There's a thought." Miss Murdoch rinsed the glasses and stacked them in the draining rack.

"But it was probably just vandals."

"Perhaps."

This was hopeless! She decided on a different approach. "Miss Murdoch, do you remember, last Monday, some people came around to the door, trick-or-treating?"

"Let me see. There were one or two, I seem to recall. Then I ran out of candy and had to turn them away. Why do you ask?"

"Well"—Hannah blushed—"three of them were Sam Fallon, Susie, and, um, me. Only you didn't recognize us because we had masks on."

"Dear me. Really? Well, you're quite right, I had no idea it was you, but I hope you were among the lucky ones who got the treats?"

"Oh yes. Thank you. I mean, please don't take this the wrong way, but when we saw you we, we couldn't help noticing that you were, well . . ." She trailed off.

"That I was what?"

"That you were wearing a long robe," she replied lamely.

"I was entertaining guests for dinner. Is that so unusual?"

"No. Of course not. I'm sorry. We must have interrupted you."

"You did, but that was hardly your fault. I opened the door."

"And you said some things we didn't understand. Words that sounded like—" She stopped, red with embarrassment.

"Words that sounded like what?"

Hannah swallowed hard. It was no good—she was just going to have to be direct. "Miss Murdoch, are you—do you—know anything at all about witchcraft?"

There. She had said it now. There was no going back.

Miss Murdoch dried her hands on a towel hanging over the oven rail and turned around. "I think the question you are trying to ask me, Hannah, is, am I a witch? Is that right?" Her eyes no longer looked timid and mouselike. They were watchful and considering, like a cat's. Hannah was the mouse now.

"No!"

"Are you sure?"

Hannah felt desperate. Millie had been kind, hadn't she? Giving up her free time to tutor her. And now she'd insulted her. Worse than that, it must seem like she was accusing her! She wanted the kitchen floor to swallow her up.

But the teacher was frowning now with concentration. "Sit down, Hannah."

Hannah did as she was told and waited. A quarter of a minute passed in silence; a silence broken only by the ticking of the pendulum clock on the wall. Then Millie began to speak.

"I don't approve of these modern shenanigans at Halloween," she said severely, "but I dislike keeping the door barred, just in case . . . at any rate, you are quite right, I am a witch. A Wiccan witch."

Hannah held her breath.

"Let me explain," began Miss Murdoch. "Wicca, or witchcraft if you prefer, is simply . . . a craft. A wisdom. We who practice it like to celebrate the ancient festivals, to study the old pagan rituals, to perform a little harmless magic, mostly to do with healing and protecting and so on. We attempt to understand the endless cycle of the seasons, and to be one with the Great Earth Mother!"

If the math lesson hadn't been confusing, this

certainly was. Millie's activities sounded like a particularly eccentric kind of alternative medicine.

"You mean you're a . . . a . . . good witch?"

Miss Murdoch sighed. Then she got up, opened a cupboard and took down a little brown pharmacist's bottle. Hannah viewed it in alarm.

"There's no need to worry—these are the pills I take for my heart." She unscrewed the top and shook out a couple into the palm of her hand. "Listen. If I feel unwell, I take two of these with a glass of water. If, however, I wanted to kill myself, I would probably take the contents of the whole bottle, washed down with something much stronger! The tablets haven't changed, only my intentions toward them."

Hannah looked blank.

"You see, magic is like this bottle of pills. Used with care, it does no harm, even a little good. But used the wrong way—" She stopped, and Hannah frowned.

"I think I see," she said. She felt that they were straying from the point. "But does that have anything to do with the stolen statue?"

Miss Murdoch said nothing at first. Then she seemed to make up her mind about something.

"Those statues are made from oak," she said at

117

last. "It may well be that the tree they came from was already many hundreds of years old even before they were carved. Its roots might have lain deep in the earth since the times when our pagan ancestors worshipped the tree spirits and believed in their power to protect them. The oak was revered above all other trees for its magic and its strength. It is said that when an oak tree is felled, it screams, like a person!"

Hannah shivered. "But . . . the statues are more than just . . . lumps of wood? Even magic wood! They could work miracles once. Couldn't they?"

"Magic and miracles!" muttered Miss Murdoch, a hint of contempt creeping into her voice. "These are just words. Words that men use to show their disapproval of one and their reverence for the other. That is why witches have always been persecuted but priests respected. In the end, there is only one word—wisdom!"

It was still very quiet in the little kitchen, but something had changed in the quality of the silence.

"You have made some kind of connection with those statues, haven't you, Hannah?"

For the first time, Hannah forced herself to consider this, and knew that Miss Murdoch was right. "I drew them," she said sadly. "That's all."

"I see."

If Hannah had looked up at that moment, she might have noticed a subtle alteration in the teacher's expression. But she was staring down at the table.

"There is something else troubling you, isn't there?"

"Yes," replied Hannah slowly. "It was something you said. When you stood on the doorstep and gave us the candy. You said, 'Remember, on this night the veil between the worlds is at its thinnest!' What did you mean by that?"

Miss Murdoch frowned. "It is perhaps hard to believe, in these days of bright lights, of fast cars, of television and horror movies, that at one time our ancestors would have regarded the Eve of All Hallows very differently from how we have come to see it now. Today it is little more than an excuse for a party. A bit of rowdy behavior. A century or so ago no right-minded people would have ventured out on such a night, let alone allowed their children to do so!"

"What exactly were they afraid of?"

"They knew that on this night the dead revisit the earth," replied Miss Murdoch simply. "And they were afraid to meet them as they walked."

"But no one believes that anymore, do they? Not

now?" Hannah was aware of the pleading in her own voice. She didn't want to hear any of this.

"What people believe is not always the point."

An uncomfortable silence followed this remark. Hannah suddenly noticed what was different about this silence. Something was missing. What was it? Then she realized. The clock had stopped ticking.

She looked at her watch. "Oh no! It's almost eight! I must go. Thanks very much for your help, and for . . . everything else."

"You are very welcome," replied the teacher, showing her pupil to the front door and watching her down the path.

✦ CHAPTER TWELVE ✦

THE CONTEST

HANNAH HAD ANOTHER BAD NIGHT. She dreamed that she was in the city during the war, watching a house burning down and powerless to stop it. Firemen were training hoses on the blaze, but with no effect. The flames leaped higher and higher; it was almost as if the fire gathered strength from the force of the water directed against it. And above the crackling and the shouts and the noise of falling timbers, she could make out the sound of a baby crying. She knew that the baby was inside the building, but when she tried to tell the firemen, no sound would come from her mouth.

At last she woke up, convinced she could smell burning. Then she opened her eyes and went cold with fear. Standing very black and still against the door was a cloaked and hooded figure! Her shaking, desperate fingers searched for the bedside lamp, and just as she thought she would faint from terror she found the switch and flooded the room with light. But all she could see was her bathrobe hanging on the bedroom door.

So it seemed like an extension of the nightmare when Miss Rycroft came up to her at the beginning of morning break and told her that Mr. Andrade wanted to see her again.

"Oh no!" She looked at the teacher in alarm, but Miss Rycroft only shrugged sympathetically and walked off.

"It's bound to be that policeman again," she said unhappily to Sam.

"Hannah Price! The Boldest, The Meanest, The Most Hardened Criminal of Our Time!" he muttered in the deep, gravelly whisper of a movie advertisement.

"Oh shut up!"

"Ladies and gentlemen, what you are about to see will thrill you to your—"

"Shut *up*!"

"Don't worry," he called as she was on her way out of the classroom. "If they lock you up I can come and visit you and Dad at the same time. I'll save a bus fare!"

For the second time in four days Hannah made her way down the corridor to the principal's office and knocked on the door.

"Come in!" she heard after a short pause.

She pushed open the door and edged around it, hardly daring to look to see who was there. But to her astonishment there was no Sergeant Bean. Instead, Miss Beamish, the art teacher, was sitting chatting to Mr. Andrade, and as Hannah appeared, they both looked up, smiling.

"Ah, Hannah! Come in and sit down. No need to look so terrified!"

Mr. Andrade seemed to have forgotten that it was only last Tuesday that she had had every reason to look terrified, but Hannah allowed herself to feel relieved, at least for the time being. She edged farther into the room and sat down rather uncomfortably on a chair between the two teachers.

"I expect you are wondering why I sent for you," began Mr. Andrade, smiling coyly.

Hannah wasn't sure if she was supposed to reply to this, so she nodded and smiled back. When were they all going to stop grinning at one another and come to the point? She might not be in trouble over the statues right now, but on the other hand she couldn't remember doing anything particularly good lately, certainly nothing for them both to look so delighted about.

"I have a letter here from A.com.o.data, a computer firm," said Mr. Andrade at last, showing her a sheet of paper. "They have written to me to say that they are sponsoring an interschool art contest, for which the first prize is two thousand pounds' worth of computer equipment for the winning school and three hundred pounds for the individual to spend on art materials!" Again he smiled at her, but as Hannah continued to look bewildered, he went on:

"Now ideally we should really stage our own competition within the school first of all, so that everyone has a chance, but as the entries must be submitted by the middle of next month—and as you know, this is an exceptionally busy semester for us—Miss Beamish has suggested that we choose one person to represent the whole school, and she feels that you are the most suitable!" This speech was followed by another dazzling smile.

"But . . . I'm only in middle school!" blurted Hannah in astonishment. "What about all the people in the years above me?"

"The thing is, Hannah," explained Miss Beamish,

"the company has specified a head-and-shoulders portrait, and there is no one else in this school who comes close to your ability to draw faces."

Hannah was silent, stupefied.

"You should be pleased, you know," said Mr. Andrade, slightly reprovingly.

"Oh, of course! I'm sorry . . . I didn't mean to sound ungrateful! It's just that . . . well, it's a surprise. That's all."

"The other reason we chose you is because the portrait must be in oils, and I think you have some experience with oil painting, don't you?" asked Miss Beamish.

"Yes, a little," she admitted. "I got oil paints for my last birthday, and my uncle showed me how to use them. I've done quite a lot of experimenting on my own, but I think I might need some help."

"Don't worry, I can spend some extra time with you, and all your art classes between now and the end of next month can be spent practicing. Oh, and we forgot to say you can choose your own model. Anyone you like, provided they agree, of course!"

"And I trust you will agree to be the chosen artist?" enquired Mr. Andrade.

"Oh, yes, of course. I mean, thank you very much," stammered Hannah. She had turned pink from embarrassment and was relieved when the principal stood up and told her she was free to go.

She was about to leave for home at the end of the day when she noticed a little group of people milling round the bulletin board and wandered over to see what they were looking at.

How Can You Do More For The Elderly This Xmas?

The sign was stuck in the place reserved for old people's visiting lists, and Hannah looked at it with interest.

Join Our Cooking Club And Bake These Delicious Gingerbread Babies!

Beneath this a recipe had been handwritten, with a carefully drawn picture of a gingerbread cookie in the shape of a baby, with a round head, arms straight out at right angles and knees bent outward with the feet joined at the center. At the bottom of the notice was a further message of encouragement.

Help A Neighbor Now! At Home!
(Perfect Recipe Ideas, Call Emma, 019503632)

Hannah smiled. She wondered how Mrs. Abbott would react to a batch of freshly baked gingerbread babies. Probably with disapproval, she thought, but there was no reason why she shouldn't use the recipe to make round cookies; presumably the mixture would do for either. Or she could take down the number offered and get some different ideas. Anything to make visiting the old lady less like a trip to the dentist.

She started to copy down the number when Sam appeared at her elbow and peered at the notice. "Don't bother doing that," he said. "Number's wrong. City phone numbers have all got ten digits. That one's only nine."

"Oh, well," she said, discouraged. "Never mind. I'll just make a photocopy of this recipe, though."

The little group of people had now dispersed, so she unpinned the notice from the board and was about to take it into the school office when she noticed Tabitha Trelawney standing a little way off, her dark eyes narrowed in something between a frown and a scowl.

"I'm only going to copy this," Hannah told her hurriedly. "I'll put it back as soon as I've finished."

But Tabitha said nothing. She stood, staring at the two of them until they turned away and went into the school office where the staff were preparing to leave.

"I wonder what's got into her," said Hannah. "Did she think I was trying to steal the recipe or something?"

"Who cares? She and her weird friends probably eat babies for breakfast!"

"Yuk!"

"So they didn't arrest you then, this morning." Sam grinned at her as she positioned the sheet and closed the lid of the copier.

"What? Oh! No. It wasn't the police anyway."

"Who, then?"

"Tell you in a minute. Shall I run off two of these and you can give one to your mom?"

"Okay. Might as well."

When they came out of the office, Emily and Mr. Cristanthi were standing near the front door, deep in conversation. They glanced at Hannah and she had the uncomfortable impression that they were discussing her. Sure enough, while she was replacing the recipe, Emily left, and Mr. Cristanthi walked over to the notice board.

"Emily tells me you have been feeling over-whelmed," he said with a smile. "We can't have that! I hope it isn't my history project that has over-loaded you?"

"Oh no. Not really. Though I haven't quite fin-ished it yet, I'm afraid," she said, sincerely hoping that he wouldn't press her far enough to discover that she hadn't quite started it either.

"And which building have you chosen to research?"

"What?"

"The cathedral," said Sam quickly.

Hannah's jaw dropped and she stared at him in alarm.

"She's writing about the cathedral. We were just talking about it when you came along."

"Excellent! No shortage of material there, I should imagine. And you, Sam? What is your subject?"

"The police station," he replied, smiling inno-cently. "As it happens, I've been able to do quite a lot of research there already."

"Well, well, it sounds as though you have both gotten a good start. If you need to discuss anything with me, I am available any day after school in the history room."

He glanced at the notice board and seemed to see the Cooking Club announcement for the first time. He frowned. "Oddly worded, don't you think? Why not '*for* perfect recipe ideas'? And who is Emma, I wonder?" He smiled and shrugged. "It is time to go home. Are you walking to the bus stop?"

They nodded.

"Then I will walk with you, if I may."

The three of them set off in a slightly constrained silence. Neither Sam nor Hannah could think of anything to talk about, but Mr. Cristanthi eventually started to chat about the weather.

"Have you noticed how the days are getting so much shorter now? The evenings are colder. Time to get out the winter coats, I think."

He glanced at Hannah, who smiled back politely. Grown-ups were always making remarks of this sort, but there didn't seem to be much point in replying to anything so obvious.

"I couldn't help noticing that you were wearing a very warm red jacket the other day," he said, smiling at her. "You should wear it more often. The color suits you."

Fortunately, Mr. Cristanthi's bus was already waiting at the stop, and he left them to get on before Hannah had a chance to blush.

Sam could hardly contain his delight. "You've made a hit there! 'You should wear red more often, my dear,'" he mimicked. "'The color suits you.'"

"Matches my acne, he means," said Hannah gloomily. "And by the way, thanks very much for landing me with the cathedral. Now I've got the biggest, most complicated building in the whole city to research."

"What do you mean?" He sounded hurt. "Somebody had to say something and you were just going to stand there looking dumb! Anyway, I've done you a favor. This way we've got an excuse to go and find out more about why that statue was stolen."

"We?"

"Sure. I'm looking forward to getting into some devil worship!"

She sighed. The idea of trying to put together a serious historical survey with Sam trying to turn the whole thing into a Gothic thriller was not a prospect she relished. She decided to change the subject.

"How would you feel about having your portrait painted?"

He looked deeply suspicious. "Who by?"

"Me."

"Why?"

"For a competition. A.com.o.data are offering two thousand pounds' worth of equipment for the winning entry."

He whistled, impressed at last. "Two grand? You're kidding!"

She told him about the interview with Mr. Andrade and Miss Beamish.

"And they've picked you out of everyone in this school? That's cool. Really cool!" He gave her a look of frank admiration.

"Don't hold your breath—I haven't won yet, and I'm not likely to either. I haven't had nearly enough experience with oil painting and there are about six hundred schools in the contest, but it could be some fun. I can choose any model I like as long as they say yes, and if I paint you, we can do it during the weekends and after school and things. In fact if you come over to my house this Sunday afternoon I'll start some practice sketches and my mom will cook for us."

The look of suspicion had returned. "I'm not going to have to dress up in a velvet suit and a lacy collar or anything dumb like that?"

Hannah giggled. "Well, I could paint you as Little Lord Fauntleroy, I suppose, but I'm not sure I could make it very convincing!"

"Good. Then I'll wear my soccer uniform."

"All right. It's only a head-and-shoulders portrait so I don't expect it matters what you wear. We can talk about all that on Sunday."

"What will we eat?" Sam had experience with Hannah's mom's cooking.

"I'll make sure it's something normal."

"No brown rice?"

"No brown rice."

"And no homemade vegetable soup?"

"I'll tell her to make it as unhealthy as possible," she promised him solemnly.

"Okay then."

Hannah sighed. "I bet Rembrandt never had this much trouble persuading his models to sit for him."

"Who?"

"Never mind."

CHAPTER THIRTEEN

HISTORY LESSON

ON SATURDAY MORNING, Susie called to say that she would visit Mrs. Abbott that day to make up for last week, and Hannah found herself unexpectedly free. Reluctantly, she decided to begin her history project. But where to start? If only Sam had thought of somewhere else! She shuddered at the thought of the sheer quantity of literature on the subject. Maybe Dad could help her to figure it all out.

But when she found him in the living room he was surrounded by a litter of cardboard packing, small plastic bags, and assorted planks of wood. On the floor beside him was a sheet of paper with writing and small diagrams, above which was a picture of a man holding a screwdriver and looking pleased with himself.

Her father on the other hand looked far from happy. "Can you see another of these anywhere?" he asked her, holding up a small screw with a bolt attached to one end. "There should be eight, but I can only find seven."

Hannah bent down and scanned the rug closely. "What's all this going to be when it's finished?"

"CD cabinet. Easy to assemble. That's what it says on the box, anyway. Not so easy to assemble if you haven't got enough screws." He peered underneath a chair and shook his head. "Any luck?"

"No."

"It can't have been packed right then. Oh well, can't do anything more till I've got all the pieces." He stood up and immediately looked happier. Rather like the man on the instruction sheet in fact, thought Hannah, smiling to herself.

"Since you can't finish that, will you help me out with my history project?"

He glanced briefly at the chaos on the floor. "Only if I can persuade your mother that it's more important than going to the hardware store."

"No problem. We have to choose one of the city buildings that wasn't destroyed in the war, and try and say why. Sam's doing the police station. He says if he'd had any say it'd have been the first place to be blown up!"

Dad smiled wryly. "What about you?"

"I'm doing the cathedral. The trouble is, it's so big and so old, I'm not sure where to start."

Her father sat down, putting his elbows on the arms of the chair and placing his hands together so that only the tips of his fingers touched. "It's interesting to consider why the cathedral survived undamaged. It would have been a big-enough target!"

"Maybe the Germans thought it would be bad luck to destroy it."

"Superstition, you mean?"

"Perhaps. I don't know."

"Or could it have been protected, I wonder. From the inside."

Hannah swallowed. She didn't want to go down this road.

"You see," went on William Price thoughtfully, "that building has survived a great deal more than bombs. Once, it was the center of a huge monastery." He paused to gaze out of the window. "It would have been a busy, bustling kind of place. The monks didn't just spend their time praying and reading the Bible and writing manuscripts in pretty colors, you know."

She sighed. Oh well, she'd asked for a history lesson, and now it looked as though she was going to get one.

"The Benedictines were very active. They nursed the sick, fed the poor, educated children, and generally made themselves useful. No one who came to them for help was ever turned away. They were known as the 'Black Order,' because they wore black habits."

Hannah felt a shiver go down her spine as she remembered the hooded figures in the alleyway beside the cathedral. But they had simply turned out to be wearing raincoats. Hadn't they? She frowned and tried to concentrate. "So if they were so useful, what happened? Why isn't the monastery there anymore?"

"King Henry the Eighth got tired of his wife and decided he wanted a divorce. The trouble was, as well as being king he was also head of the church, so he wasn't allowed to have one. That meant he had to choose between the church and a new wife."

"So what did he do?"

"He chose a new wife. The Roman Catholic Church had to go, and a new church was created. The monasteries were destroyed, the statues burned, and the silver and gold were melted down and made into coins so that Henry wouldn't be short of money."

"And people just let him do it?"

"They had no choice. To publicly disagree with the king was seen as treason, and treason carried the death penalty. Besides . . ." He paused.

"What?"

"Well, it wasn't quite so simple as I've made it sound. When I said that the Benedictines made themselves useful, that was true of some houses. Maybe not all." Her father nibbled his thumb thoughtfully.

"What do you mean?"

He stopped nibbling his thumb and scratched his head instead. "There were tales of corrupt practices in some of the monasteries, mostly just overindulgence of one sort or another but occasionally more serious than that."

Her eyes widened. "Crime, you mean?"

"Nowadays it would be called taking money under false pretences. Many of the monasteries possessed what were known as holy relics. Bones of saints, fragments of the True Cross, that kind of thing. They almost certainly weren't genuine, but people didn't want to take any risks with their chances of forgiveness for sins they had committed and were prepared to pay good money if they were allowed to touch the things."

"Yuk!" Hannah wrinkled her nose in distaste.

"Quite. Now it would probably be dismissed as just a lot of superstitious nonsense, but then, once the new church was established, those practices were seen as heresy, which also carried the death penalty because it went against the wishes of the king, who was still head of the church. Superstition was linked with witchcraft, and one or two of the monks were even accused of having sold their souls to the devil in return for immortality!"

Hannah shivered, suddenly reminded for some reason of the dark, hooded figure standing against her bedroom door. Then she shook her head, ridding it of the image. It had only been her bathrobe, for goodness' sake!

"You mean it was a crime to be superstitious? You could be put to death for crossing your fingers or not walking under ladders?" She smiled faintly.

"It was a crime to worship objects."

"Like the Virgin and Child, you mean?" She stopped smiling and frowned. "But then why . . . ?"

"Why didn't they destroy the statues? I imagine they must have been hidden, don't you think?

Until all the fuss died down and things were calmer."

"I suppose so." She sat for a while in thoughtful silence. Then she turned back to her father. "But when the king died, couldn't they just rebuild the monasteries?"

"Oh, by that time everybody had got themselves into a state. Some people wanted to keep the new faith, some stuck to the old, and for the next two hundred years they continued to torture and murder one another, all in the name of religion! A lot of people escaped to the New World—to America. To get away from it all."

"But why?" asked Hannah. "It doesn't seem worth fighting about."

"Some people," her father said slowly, "might say they were afraid. Afraid of what would happen to them if they chose the wrong side."

"Superstition again?"

Her father didn't answer this question. Instead he said, "People were ignorant about a lot of things then. They didn't know much about science and medicine. They needed to believe that someone was taking care of them."

Hannah dimly began to see where this long history lesson might be leading. "I suppose, in the old days," she said, "that's why they wanted to believe that the Virgin and Child could work miracles. They wanted to be taken care of?"

Again her father didn't reply directly. "I've always believed that the best way to stop being afraid of the unknown is by acquainting oneself with as many facts as possible." He looked closely at his daughter, and she shifted uncomfortably.

"Was that meant for me?"

"Well, you are afraid, aren't you?" he said gently. "Afraid of what happened last week?"

She looked at the floor. Then she raised her eyes and looked at her father. She sighed. "I'm still not sure where to start."

"As a historian, I should urge you to begin with a primary source," he said solemnly.

"An original document, you mean? Where on earth am I going to get one of those?"

"Perhaps you should construct one of your own."

"How?" she demanded.

"Didn't this all start with a picture?"

Which was why, at three o'clock that afternoon, Hannah found herself seated on a slatted wooden bench facing the south wall of the cathedral, unenthusiastically sketching. She didn't particularly like drawing buildings—all that angle and perspective felt a bit too much like geometry—but she recognized that it was something that would probably earn her marks, and in any case it was a good way of filling space without having to do too much writing.

She worked steadily for half an hour, then stopped for a rest. It was while she was gazing idly about her, watching the visitors come and go, that she noticed the day chaplain. He was walking in her direction. Hannah's first instinct was to get up and quietly walk away. She certainly wasn't in the mood for any more interrogation, but the man had clearly seen her and seemed to be making straight for her. It was too late to escape now.

"I thought it was you! As soon as I saw someone sitting there, scribbling away, I felt sure it must be you!" said the chaplain, approaching rather breathlessly.

She said nothing, unable to deny that it was her.

"I'm afraid I owe you an apology," he said, shaking his head. "When the police came and started asking questions, I . . . we were all very upset because of the theft, and when they asked me if I could recollect anything unusual happening . . . someone taking a close interest . . . well, I'm afraid I immediately thought of you."

"It's okay. It wasn't your fault. You must have thought I was a bit strange!"

"To be honest, I wasn't thinking straight. It was all such a shock, you see. We were about to close up the cathedral after the evening congregation had left, and that was when I noticed the statue was missing. Then on top of it all there was that woman taken ill—"

"What woman?"

"Another of the staff here. Poor thing became very sick. I wanted to call an ambulance but she said she would just go home and rest. The next thing I heard, she'd been admitted to the hospital. She'd had a stroke! Anyway"—he looked at her anxiously—"I do hope you didn't get into too much trouble over what I said?"

"It's all right. I told them where I was last Saturday afternoon and I think they can check it."

"Well, that's good." The man looked relieved. "I don't suppose there is anything I can do for you to make up for it? I see you are sketching the cathedral."

"Actually," said Hannah as a thought struck her, "you could help me. I'm trying to get some information for a project I'm working on. Is there a plan of the building . . . a guidebook or something?"

"Certainly there is! Any special aspect you're interested in?"

She looked blank and was about to say no, when she thought it might sound better if she could pretend to be interested in something in particular, so she asked if there was a plan of the original monastery buildings.

"I'm afraid there is no plan like that in the church itself . . . you would have to go to the cathedral bookshop for that," he told her regretfully. "But I can show you where the boundary wall lay, if you would care to let me?"

Hannah couldn't very well say no, and in any case she was bored with sketching, so she stood up and allowed herself to be led on a leisurely walk around the edge of the cathedral courtyard, with the chaplain enthusiastically pointing out the original site of the gatehouse, the infirmary, the refectory, the monks' cemetery, and the vegetable gardens.

There was nothing much left to see apart from a few stones to mark where the ancient buildings had once stood, and Hannah soon found her mind wandering from what the chaplain was telling her. Every so often she was jolted back to attention when he turned to face her, and she did her best to look interested.

"And this was the outer parlor, where the porter sat who kept the cloister door."

She nodded dutifully.

"And here would have been the bakehouse and the kitchen. Beneath would have been cellars and storehouses for provisions."

At last they stopped in front of a single-story building of redbrick.

"And this was the almonry, where the monks distributed alms to the poor and looked after the sick people of the parish."

"But this doesn't look old enough to be part of the cathedral," Hannah pointed out.

"Quite right," said the chaplain, smiling with approval. "It was put up by the Victorians at the end of the nineteenth century, but the floor is the original stone of the old building. Let me show you."

He led the way down two stone steps and opened a narrow door. Hannah followed him and found herself in a long, high-ceilinged room with a large brick fireplace at one end. At the other end four rows of chairs were set out, with two rows facing the other two. A row of pegs held red choir robes, and a battered bookcase contained an even more battered collection of hymnbooks and sheet music.

"This is used by the boys in the choir school now for their practices," the chaplain told her. "While they sing, they stand on nine centuries of history!"

He frowned suddenly and looked at his watch. "Good heavens! It's nearly time for evensong. I must get back to the cathedral! Will you walk back with me or do you want to stay here?"

"I'll come back. I need to get home."

As they exited the building, Hannah turned left to retrace their steps, but the chaplain stopped her. "We'll go around this way, if you don't mind. Bad luck to walk around a church widdershins!"

"Widdershins?"

"Counterclockwise. Just a lot of irreligious superstition, but I don't believe in taking any chances, especially not with all this flu about!"

They followed the line of the ancient monastery wall, now approaching the west door from the north. Hannah noticed an elegant, comfortable-looking house in mellow redbrick with a well-kept lawn in front of it. "What's that?" she asked.

"That's where the bishop lives. He's the boss, as you might say."

"You mean the head of the cathedral?"

"I suppose so. I'm not sure that's quite how he would describe it!" The chaplain chuckled. "I think he sees himself more as a kind of caretaker."

Hannah frowned. She imagined someone wearing overalls and carrying a toolbox, like the caretaker did at Manningham. "He must have been very upset when the statue was stolen, then. If he thought he was meant to be taking care of it."

The man gave her a curious look. "Upset! More than upset I should say," he murmured. "He's heartbroken. You'd think it was his own child, almost. Now, here we are. I must go inside and you must be going home. I hope I have been able to help you with your work?"

"Oh yes! Thank you. It's been . . . great."

She said good-bye and thankfully escaped. She had had more than enough history for one day.

On Sunday morning, Sam arrived wearing his entire soccer uniform.

"We'll go into the dining room," Hannah told him as soon as he had said hello to her mother and they were alone again. "There's good light in there and no one will disturb us. There's something I've got to tell you."

She settled him on a chair in front of the window,

drew up another opposite, and picked up her sketch pad, which was ready waiting on the table. Sam immediately took on a pained, unnatural expression, as if he were sitting on a thumbtack.

"You all right?" asked Hannah curiously.

"Yeah. Why?"

"You look as if you've got a stomachache."

"No, I'm okay." A self-conscious and faintly idiotic smile appeared on his face.

"You don't have to pose for this, you know. Anyway, do you really think you could go on looking like that for an hour at a time? I just need you to look natural. Normal."

"I don't know what I look like normally!" He scowled at her.

"That's better!" Hannah laughed. "At least it's a look I recognize!"

For twenty minutes or so she worked in silence, sketching in outlines, rubbing out, trying to get the shape of the face and the bone structure exactly right. It was much harder drawing Sam than Emily. Emily's features were more regular, her expression far less mobile than Sam's, whose face seemed to change every time she looked at him.

"I went to see Millie Murdoch on Thursday," she said at last, shading the line of his jaw.

"Oh yeah? Find anything out? Or did she wipe your memory clean?"

Hannah shook her head. "She's completely different when she hasn't got a whole class to control. Calm and—well—sane, really. I think she probably ought to have been a governess or something like that. She doesn't have any trouble teaching one person on their own."

"Is that all you wanted to tell me?"

"No. It wasn't the math. It was what she said afterward." She gave him a brief account of what Miss Murdoch had said, then watched his reaction. His face was skeptical and amused.

Hannah stared. That was it! The good-humored but mocking eyes, the slight smile around the corners of the mouth, that was exactly the expression she needed to capture for her portrait. Her pencil raced excitedly, and she hardly listened to what he was saying.

"I told you she was crazy! And she's doing her best to make you crazy too. If she didn't confuse you with math, she certainly did it with all that stuff about tree spirits and earth mothers. The trouble with you is you've got that statue on the brain and you can't think straight. You've just got to forget about it and get on with your life!"

This was the longest speech she had ever heard from Sam, and she knew that some of it at least was true. She had got the statue on the brain, and she couldn't think straight as a result. But the one thing she wasn't able to do was to forget about it.

CHAPTER FOURTEEN

THE BREAK-IN

FOR THE NEXT TEN DAYS she was too absorbed in the painting to give much thought to anything else. The image of the statue was still there, but more in the background of her mind, while the foreground was filled with plans for Sam's portrait. Miss Beamish had presented her with a stretched and primed canvas.

"Normally, you should prepare a canvas yourself," she said, "but as time is short I've bought this one ready-made." She showed Hannah how to mix the oil paint with turpentine in different proportions according to what kind of texture she wanted, and explained how to build up the painting layer by layer.

"The great thing about oils is that because they

take time to dry, you can change things the next day if you don't like them. That way you get a second chance."

Most of the class was enthusiastic about the painting, and eager to watch its progress. Emily in particular spent more time watching Hannah than she did on her own work. Sam was horribly self-conscious at first, but soon got over it when he realized that people were more interested in the picture itself than in him.

Only two things slightly disturbed Hannah during this time, and the first could, she thought, have been just her imagination.

"Sam," she said to him one morning as they were getting out their books for morning classes, "did you borrow anything from my desk?"

"No. Why? Something missing?"

She shook her head. "Doesn't seem to be."

"Then what's the problem?"

"My pencil case isn't where I left it. I always put it at the front of my desk. Now it's at the back."

Sam, whose own desk would have made a trash can look neat, shrugged impatiently. "So? Someone probably wanted to borrow a textbook or something."

"Maybe. I think I noticed it the day before yesterday too."

He shrugged again. "If you haven't lost anything, who cares?"

The other thing happened a few days later, as they were leaving school. Emily approached Sam and Hannah, looking worried.

"I've just seen Millie Murdoch talking to Tabitha in the coatroom. I'm not sure, but it sounded as if Millie had caught her looking in people's pockets."

"What's she want to do that for?" asked Sam scornfully. "Her folks are loaded!"

"I suppose it does seem a bit unlikely," admitted Emily. "I may have misheard what they were saying."

"Why are you telling us, anyway?" demanded Sam.

"Well," said Emily, sounding even more worried. She looked at Hannah. "It's just that they were standing right next to the peg where you hang your coat."

Alarmed, Hannah put her hands in her pockets and found her wallet and her house keys. She unzipped the wallet and peered inside, trying to remember how much she'd had in there. "Seems okay," she said, frowning.

"Oh well, that's a relief." Emily smiled at her. "I expect I just jumped to conclusions!"

But apart from these two small incidents, Hannah's mind was on painting. The time passed satisfyingly, and she looked forward to each day as an opportunity to build on what she had done before. Sometimes the paint wasn't dry enough for her to continue and she grew impatient and frustrated, but after a while she accepted the waiting as part of the process and used the time to do some careful planning on the next stage.

Then on Friday, November the eighteenth, something happened after school that made her forget all about Sam's portrait for the time being.

As soon as she saw the police car parked outside the gate, she knew something was wrong, but it wasn't until she let herself in and saw her father talking to Sergeant Bean that she realized that this time it didn't seem to be her fault.

"I'm afraid it's bad news, Hannah," said Dad. "We've had a break-in."

She peered in through the door to the living room and gasped. Every book had been taken out of the bookcase and thrown to the ground, every ornament had been removed from the mantelpiece and put on some other surface, sometimes the floor, sometimes a table. The chairs had been pulled out into the middle of the room, their cushions scattered and the loose covers half pulled off. There seemed to be nothing in the room that hadn't been touched, yet curiously, nothing seemed to be broken and she couldn't see anything missing.

A young man in uniform stood beside the fireplace.

"This is Detective Constable Clutterbuck. He's, um, assisting me." Sergeant Bean sounded as though he wasn't expecting much in the way of assistance however, and in spite of her alarm Hannah thought she could see why. The young constable was tall and thin, with ears that stood out almost at right angles from a face that wore an expression of contented serenity, which under the circumstances verged on imbecility. He was examining a patch of wallpaper that had been neatly cut to expose some electrical wires that had previously made a slight bulge on the wall.

"This shouldn't be too hard to repair," he was telling Mrs. Price. "You just need to wet the edges of the paper and stick them back with a dab of glue. Once it dries it'll be as good as new." He smiled encouragingly.

"All right, Clutterbuck, this is a criminal

investigation, not a lesson in interior decorating!" muttered Sergeant Bean.

But Mom wasn't listening to either of them. She was gazing hopelessly at the chaos. "They've even taken the lids off all my saucepans!" She turned to Hannah, palms upraised, tears spilling over. "Why? What on earth did they think they'd find there?"

"One thing seems quite clear," Sergeant Bean was saying. "These weren't regular housebreakers, or they wouldn't have left the video or the stereo or that computer you've got there. Those are simple things to get rid of."

"You mean, they didn't take anything?" Hannah said in disbelief. "Nothing at all?"

Her father looked unhappy. "I think you'd better see for yourself. Come upstairs." He led the way to her bedroom, with Hannah and the Sergeant following.

From the doorway she saw a scene of complete turmoil. Every drawer was open, with clothes either spilling out or strewn over the floor. A little papier-mâché box that had held beads and tiny toys from past Christmas crackers and one or two foreign coins lay upside down in the middle of the carpet. Even the battered green folder that she'd hidden behind the bookcase had been discovered, the drawings roughly stuffed back.

Then she saw her bed. On the rumpled quilt lay three teddy bears, a panda, a white rabbit with buckteeth, a small black dog of unknown breed, and a ginger cat. Every one of them had been savagely ripped open, and they lay in horribly unnatural positions: some turned nearly inside out, others with limbs hanging by a few threads. It was like looking at the shocking aftermath of a massacre.

She sat on the bed and picked up the panda. A little pile of stuffing fell onto her lap. Like blood, she thought. Toy blood.

"I'm sorry, sweetheart." Dad sat down beside her and put his arm around her. "This must be a terrible shock for you."

"It's okay." Helpless tears had begun to roll down her cheeks, and she brushed them away impatiently with the back of her hand. "Mom hasn't taken it very well either, has she?"

"Well, when you think of the fuss she makes when I fold the newspaper untidily, I suppose it's only natural she should get a bit upset when a human tornado rampages through her house leaving a trail of devastation behind it! But at least it can be cleared up in time. Whereas your toys are a different thing altogether."

The sound of a throat being cleared behind them made them turn around. They had forgotten about Sergeant Bean.

"I don't suppose you've any idea, any idea at all, what this person . . . people might have been after?" He was looking at Hannah, not her father.

She shook her head.

"Anything missing that you can see?"

"I . . . don't think so."

"We'll be sending someone to take fingerprints later on today. Until then, please don't touch anything. Then, when you've been able to look through everything, let us know if anything is missing."

Downstairs, Detective Constable Clutterbuck was explaining to a bewildered Mom the best way to get bloodstains out of a carpet, quite undeterred by the fact that this was one problem they didn't appear to have. He had moved on from home decorating, it seemed. Sergeant Bean sharply rounded him up and shepherded him outside.

"Can I have a quick word with you?" he murmured to Hannah, out of earshot of her parents.

She followed the two policemen out the front door.

"We've traced that social worker," he told her.

"And? She remembered me?"

The sergeant looked uncomfortable. "Unfortunately not. She remembered visiting the Fallons, of course, but didn't seem to have any recollection of you being there as well.

"I was there," she said helplessly. "Honestly!"

"Oh well, not to worry."

She swallowed hard. "He . . . they . . . can't have been searching for the statue, can they?"

"No. Not that. Something a lot smaller."

"That's what I thought."

"I don't suppose for a moment there's any connection, but if you think of anything, give me a call. Your father's got the number."

The two men got into their car and drove off, leaving Hannah to go back inside the chaotic house.

CHAPTER FIFTEEN

DISCOVERY OF A MISSING DIGIT

"YOU'RE KIDDING! They went through the whole house without taking anything?"

It was Sunday afternoon, and Sam was waiting while Hannah set up her easel and arranged tubes of paint.

"Not so much as a box of matches. You should have seen the mess, though. No stone unturned and no saucepan lid untouched! Mom's going to take weeks to get over it. Where did I put that vermilion?" She rummaged in her book bag.

"Maybe that's what they were after, a tube of paint. Someone wants to stop you from painting me!"

"Don't flatter yourself." Hannah turned the bag upside down onto the carpet. "Oh! There it is!" She began to put the rest of her things back. "What's this?" She picked up a torn, crumpled sheet of paper and examined it.

"That's that dumb recipe," said Sam, peering over her shoulder. "Those gingerbread things. You can toss it. Mom says the mixture's all wrong. Too much ginger and not enough sugar. So it's not just the phone number that's wrong. Whoever's organizing this cooking club needs help."

Hannah settled herself in front of the easel and looked thoughtfully at her work.

"So what were they looking for?"

"No idea." She began applying paint with care.

"You said someone had been in your desk."

"What? Oh, yes." She frowned and rubbed delicately with a damp rag.

"And Emily said Millie Murdoch caught Tabitha looking in your pockets."

"She said she might have been wrong about that."

"Or maybe she was right."

"Don't be stupid!" Hannah put the brush down and looked at him impatiently. "You're not suggesting that Tabitha cut school on Friday afternoon so she could do a bit of housebreaking!"

"Did you see her in school?" He grinned, and

she realized he was joking.

"Anyway, there wasn't anything in my pocket—" She broke off suddenly.

"What?"

"Oh, nothing."

"Why did you stop then?"

"I just remembered something," she said slowly. "You know that night we were out trick-or-treating, and I left you and Susie and went home by myself?"

He nodded.

"I went into the city center."

"You *what*?"

"All right, all right. I got lost. I didn't tell you because I knew you'd make fun of me for going the wrong way. The thing is, I met this old man. I thought he was a beggar and I offered him money but he didn't seem to want that."

"What did he want?"

Hannah looked at the floor. The incident had affected her like a dream, and she had almost come to believe that that was all it was. She didn't want to tell Sam about it.

"Well?"

"Just some stuff in my pocket."

"What was in there?"

"Nothing. Odds and ends of junk. A tissue."

"You mean you gave a beggar a tissue? You're kidding!"

"That was all I had. He just took it from me, looked at it, and gave it back."

"Why?"

"How should I know? He was probably just some crazy old tramp. I don't even know why I'm telling you about it!"

"Have you still got it?"

"The tissue, you mean? Are you serious?"

He nodded.

"I've no idea."

"Look in your coat and see."

She stared at him for a few seconds, then left the room. When she came back she shook her head. "It's not there. I guess I threw it away." She paused. "Wait a minute! I wasn't wearing my raincoat at Halloween because I'd lent it to Katie Brown and she hadn't given it back. I was wearing my red jacket."

"Go and get it then."

Feeling faintly ridiculous, but nevertheless curious, she went out of the room and returned a minute later carrying her jacket. "It's still here," she said, taking out the balled-up, slightly grubby-looking tissue. "I can't believe anyone would go to the trouble of stealing it though."

Sam took it from her and knelt on the floor. He shook it out, and a handful of small objects fell on the carpet. He examined the collection carefully. "Paper clip, coin, rubber band, candy wrapper and"—he peered closely—"a fossilized grub! Plus a lot of fluff. Where did you get all this?"

"I picked it up in the cathedral the day after the theft when I went back to look for my scarf. I dropped some money and it rolled behind a pillar. When I tried to get it back, that junk must have come with it. The fluff kind of held it together."

"Well, none of this stuff looks like the sort of thing anyone'd break into a house for. Unless it's the fossilized grub! Could be a rare and valuable species, I suppose. . . ." He smiled and picked it up. "No, sorry, I was wrong. It's just a bit of stick."

"That's a shame. I was hoping I might have scooped up a priceless diamond without knowing it!"

Sam didn't reply. He was staring at the tiny object. Staring hard. "Have you got a magnifying glass?"

"There's one in the car. Dad uses it to read maps."

"Go and get it." His voice was tense with excitement.

"Why?"

"Go *and get it!*"

She left the room, picked up the car keys from the hall table, and went out the front door. A minute later she was back.

Without looking up, Sam held out his hand for the magnifying glass.

"Come here."

Frowning in bewilderment, she knelt beside him on the floor and peered through the glass. Then her heart thudded against her ribs as realization flooded her brain. The piece of stick was more than just a piece of stick. It was a finger. A tiny, perfectly crafted wooden finger.

"It must have broken off!" she whispered. "When the statue was stolen. It broke and fell on the floor, and I . . . I found it. I've had it all this time and I didn't even know!"

"Someone knew."

"But how?

He shook his head slowly. "I don't know."

"Maybe it's just coincidence! Someone looking in my desk. There could have been any reason for it. Emily didn't really know if Tabitha had searched my pockets, she only thought she'd overheard something. The break-in could have had nothing to do with it!" She talked fast, feverishly, trying to convince herself and him . . . of what? She didn't want to believe the evidence of her own eyes.

"Give me that recipe."

She picked it up and he took it, smoothing out the creases and laying it flat on the floor. He examined it closely. "Could be just coincidence," he muttered. "That phone number having one digit missing could be a genuine mistake, or—"

"Or what?"

He looked up at her. "What if it's deliberate? Supposing someone's trying to get a message to someone else to tell them the statue's been broken, and they're using this cooking club as a way of communicating."

"I've no idea what you're talking about. How can you communicate using a wrong number?"

"What if it's meant to be wrong? Meant to have only nine digits instead of ten." He continued to look at her steadily, and at last the light dawned.

"You mean, to show that that's what happened to the statue? It should have ten fingers and now . . . ?"

He nodded.

"I don't believe it," she muttered. "It's too far-fetched."

"We already know the recipe doesn't work."

"Just a mistake in the quantities."

"Maybe." He turned the paper to face her. "Read it."

"I've read it. You know what it says."

"Read it out loud."

She stared at him in astonishment but did as she was told. "'How can you do more for the elderly this X-mas? Join our cooking club and bake these delicious gingerbread babies! Help a neighbor now! At home! (Perfect recipe ideas, call Emma.)' Then there's the number."

"Read the last bit again."

"Join our—"

"Not that. The bit that starts 'Help a neighbor.'"

"'Help a neighbor now! At home! (Perfect recipe ideas, call Emma.)' What's the matter?"

He was looking puzzled. "Sounds . . . weird. Unnatural. Why 'help a neighbor now, at home'? They've already said that about doing more for the elderly."

"And Mr. Cristanthi noticed something odd too," she muttered, suddenly remembering. "He pointed it out just before we walked to the bus stop." She sighed, shaking her head wearily. "I don't know. Look, Sam. D'you mind if we don't do any more on your picture today? I think I've had enough."

"Sure. I can go home." He stood up and looked

at her thoughtfully. "Listen . . . don't worry about it. Just keep that bit of wood safe. What are you going to do with it?"

"Don't know. I'll think of something."

He left, and she went back to the dining room and picked up the tiny finger. She stared at it. Was this what somebody had been so desperate to recover that they had gone to the lengths of breaking into her house to get it back? It seemed impossible! But . . .

She went upstairs to her bedroom and looked through her things for a little enamel locket given to her by an aunt for her birthday two years ago. When she found it, it was open. So that had been searched too. Carefully she put the finger inside and snapped it shut. Then she fastened it around her neck.

Later that night, when she was in bed, she looked at the cooking club notice again, slowly saying the words over and over in the hope that they might give her a clue to the mystery. Eventually she fell asleep.

CHAPTER SIXTEEN

DEAD LANGUAGE

On Monday morning she woke early and dressed with care, making sure that the little locket was hidden underneath her school blouse. When she got downstairs, her father was eating breakfast.

"What's this?" he asked through a mouthful of toast, waving a piece of paper at her.

She peered at the writing and recognized the strange words of the old man in the courtyard behind the cathedral.

"It's something someone said to me on Halloween night. It seemed to be a kind of dialect, but I couldn't make any sense of it. Where did you find it?"

"Beside your bed. We were looking through your room after the break-in, to see what might have been taken, and thought we might have found a note from the thief. It seems not though. Who said this to you?"

"Just some old tramp. Drunk, probably."

"Then why bother to write it down?"

She didn't think it was right that her father had taken something from her room without asking first, and now he was interrogating her. She decided attack was the best form of defense. "Why are you asking me about it?"

"Because it's interesting."

"You mean you know what it says?"

"Possibly."

Her heart began to beat faster. Suddenly she wasn't sure that she wanted to know what it said.

"I had to speak the words out loud to get an idea of the meaning, because obviously you just wrote down what you heard? 'Tis bitook to thee, be rayit not'?"

He pointed to her own writing and she nodded.

"Could it have sounded like this?" Here he turned the paper over so she could see the other side, where he had written: *'Tis betook to thee, bewray it not.*

"I suppose so. Yes. What does it mean?"

"It means 'It is entrusted to you, betray it not.'"

She frowned in bewilderment. "What kind of language is that, Dad?"

"It's called Middle English."

"Where is it spoken?"

"Nowhere. It's a dead language. It died out about five hundred years ago."

Hannah stared at him.

"Don't worry," Dad said reassuringly. "Halloween, was it? I expect some joker was just trying to scare you into thinking you'd met a ghost!"

Mr. Cristanthi's history class was smaller than usual. Five people were absent, including Susie and Jessica, which gave the lesson a more intimate feel. In spite of the few people, it was hot in the classroom and Hannah undid the top button on her blouse while she tried to concentrate on the lesson. Today it was about the Nazi persecution of the Jews, and Mr. Cristanthi spoke movingly of families mysteriously disappearing under cover of darkness never to be seen again, the mindless cruelty of the concentration camps, the suffocating terror of the gas chambers.

The others sat spellbound, but this time Hannah

felt her attention wandering. She couldn't get the sound of her father's words out of her head.

"It it entrusted to you, betray it not."

It was impossible now to pretend to herself that the words were meaningless. She couldn't escape the fact that for some reason the tiny scrap of wood she had had in her pocket ever since the day after the theft was important. Vital. But to what? Would it help her find the rest of the statue? It hadn't been very effective so far. And what exactly did "betray it not" mean? Don't lose it?

But what disturbed her most of all wasn't the meaning of the words; it was the language they were spoken in. Again and again she could hear her father saying, "It's a dead language. It died out about five hundred years ago."

A dead language, or the language of the dead?

She shivered, and with an effort brought her mind back to the history lesson. And now she began to notice things about Mr. Cristanthi that had previously escaped her, like the way he used his voice; one moment loud and resonant, the next a hushed whisper. His gestures were elegant and dramatic but almost too polished. Well, why not? she said to herself. Maybe being a good history teacher was a bit like being an actor. Bringing the past to life continually must get quite tedious after a while, like doing the same play night after night in the theater.

All the same, she felt vaguely uncomfortable at the way he so easily manipulated the class to feel fear, indignation, sadness, anger. It was almost as though they were all puppets and he was pulling the strings.

She was walking through the entrance hall at the end of school when she saw that the recipe was still pinned to the board. She wandered over and stared at it. No one else was looking—the notice had been up too long to attract any interest now. She sighed and moved away.

"Hannah!" She turned back to see Miss Beamish hurrying toward her. "I just thought I'd better remind you that the final date for sending off Sam's portrait is the thirteenth of next month. It will need at least a week to dry, so that means you've only got a couple more weeks."

"Oh! Okay. Thanks, Miss Beamish. I won't forget."

The teacher walked off, and Hannah was about to do the same when she glanced at the notice board once more. She was now about ten yards away, and the writing was harder to read from this distance. She could hardly make out the lower-case letters at all, in fact. Which was why the capitals stood out with more clarity.

Her heart began to beat fast as she stared at the last line. She knew it said Help A Neighbor Now! At Home! (Perfect Recipe Ideas, Call Emma).

But all she could see now was H A N N A H P R I C E.

CHAPTER SEVENTEEN

THE BISHOP

Sʜᴏᴄᴋ ᴍᴀᴅᴇ ʜᴇʀ ᴡᴇᴀᴋ. She sat down by the door in the bay reserved for visitors and stared unseeingly at a pile of magazines on a table. She needed Sam! Then she remembered. He had left school early to go with his mother and the twins to visit his father in prison. Oh, why did it have to be tonight? She felt suddenly, horribly alone. She had to talk to someone! Who then? Sergeant Bean? But he already suspected her of the theft, didn't he? This latest development might make him more suspicious still. Miss Murdoch? But Miss Murdoch was a witch. She didn't want to think about witchcraft now.

Suddenly she knew what she had to do. She got up and walked out the door, away from the school buildings, and along Tanner's Lane. When she reached the cathedral square she turned left and made her way northward from the west door until she came to the house that was now used by the choir school but had once been the site of the old almonry. Here she stopped and tried the door—not because she wanted to see the almonry again, but because she didn't want to get to where she was going before she'd had a chance to work out what she meant to say. She was hoping to have a chance to think for a few minutes. But the door was locked.

"Can I help you?" A young man in a suit and tie was walking briskly toward her.

"What?" She spun around guiltily.

"Were you looking for someone?"

"No! Well, yes. Sort of. I was, um, wondering . . . I really want to see the bishop!"

Blurted out like that it sounded ridiculous, and Hannah blushed. She felt as if she'd been caught outside Buckingham Palace announcing that she wanted to see the queen.

"The bishop is a very busy man. If you want to see him you will have to make an appointment. You may have to wait a week or so, I'm afraid." The voice was cool. "Come back tomorrow between the hours of ten and four and I'm sure they will be able to help you in the office." He gave her a small, official smile and walked off.

Bleakly she watched him go. Of course, she might have known you couldn't just visit someone as important as a bishop any old time. How could she have been so stupid! She began slowly to retrace her steps back to the west door, then remembered what the chaplain had said about not walking around a church widdershins and went back the way she'd come.

Soon she reached the elegant house of warm, crumbly brick, its tall, regular windows glinting in the remains of the afternoon sunlight. This, she knew, was where the bishop lived, and she stopped for a moment by the gate.

Just inside it an elderly red-faced man was arranging snails on a large tin tray, as if starting them off in a race. As she watched, he straightened up and she saw that he was wearing an enormous pair of corduroy trousers, torn and rather dirty, which were held up below his considerable waist by two striped ties, knotted together. She supposed he must be the gardener.

"Don't like to put salt down," he said, noticing Hannah and indicating the snail lineup. "Just collecting them so I can put them on the other side of the hedge. With any luck they won't find their way back right away!"

Hannah smiled nervously.

"Anything I can do for you, or did you just stop by for a chat?" the man enquired in a friendly voice.

"No thank you. I really wanted to see the bishop, but I can't because you have to make an appointment and it's too late to do that now."

"Delighted to meet you!" said the man, extending a grubby right hand. "I am the bishop, only"—here he hastily withdrew his hand—"don't touch me till I've had a wash! Come in, won't you, and you must tell me your name."

"Hannah. Hannah Price."

Red with embarrassment and hoping that she hadn't given away her surprise on learning that she had mistaken a bishop for a gardener, she followed the man through a side door into a large, stone-flagged kitchen with a cluttered sideboard covering half one wall and a long, scrubbed pine table holding a collection of mugs, plates, flowerpots, seed catalogues, newspapers, gloves, and more surprisingly, a Lego spaceship, half completed.

"That belongs to my grandson, Henry," explained the bishop, indicating the spaceship. "But we're stuck. I don't suppose you can see a flat square yellow piece anywhere?"

Hannah ran an eye over the spare pieces in the box, then, on a lucky hunch, picked up a flowerpot. The small yellow tile was underneath.

"Good gracious!" exclaimed Henry's grandfather. "How did you know it was there? What luck you were passing by!" He picked up a kettle and took it to the sink. "I was just about to have a cup of tea," he told her, "and I very much hope you will join me?"

"Thank you," she said. "If it's not too much trouble."

"Not at all. And as my wife is out, I think we'll help ourselves to the chocolate cookies!" He reached for a battered and rusty biscuit tin on the top shelf of the dresser. "I'm supposed to be on a diet," he explained confidentially.

"So am I," replied Hannah feelingly.

The bishop arranged the tea on a tray and led the way into a smallish room with learned-looking books lining one wall from floor to ceiling, two armchairs covered in faded flowered chintz, and a log fire crackling in the grate. On a rug in front of the fire lay what she at first took to be a small mongrel of some kind but on closer inspection turned out to be the most enormous tabby cat she had ever seen.

The bishop removed a book from one of the chairs so that she could sit down, and put the tea tray on a table between them. The cat stood up, stretched majestically, walked slowly and deliberately over to Hannah's chair, and launched itself onto her chest. For a moment or two its weight was so colossal that she almost stopped breathing. Then she cautiously shifted position till it was on her lap, where it settled itself luxuriously and started to purr like a tractor.

"I hope you don't mind cats," said the bishop. "I'm afraid Moses is rather a law unto himself!"

"Oh no! I like them," she assured him truthfully, wondering how long it would take for her left foot to go numb.

He poured two mugs of tea and offered her a cookie from the tin. Then he took one himself and sat back, nibbling contentedly and dropping crumbs on the worn Turkish rug.

"Now tell me what I can do for you!" He smiled encouragingly.

This was the moment Hannah had been dreading. Deep inside herself she knew she had come to the right place, and that if anyone could help her, this nice man could. Nevertheless, now that she had to explain the whole story, she felt weak and uncertain.

"I really don't know where to begin," she started unhappily. "It's . . . it's about the Virgin and Child."

The bishop's face clouded over. "Ah yes," he said quietly. "I see. You have something to tell me about them? About the missing baby?" For a moment a faint hope dawned in his eyes, then died again when he saw Hannah shaking her head.

As she seemed unable to continue, he said, "Why don't you begin at the beginning and tell me exactly what has brought you here today? It seems to me that you have reached a point of last resort. The clergy are often at that point, for some reason!"

Hannah cast her mind back, trying to arrange her thoughts.

"It all started with a thunderstorm," she said at last. "If it hadn't been for that, I wouldn't have lent my coat to Katie Brown and I wouldn't have had to go into the cathedral and I wouldn't have drawn the statues."

Then, as the bishop looked thoroughly baffled, she explained, as carefully and truthfully as she could, everything that had happened that day.

He now looked intrigued, so Hannah continued. This time she left nothing out. She told him about Sam, and about visiting Mrs. Abbott, and Halloween, and Miss Murdoch, and the break-in, and the cooking club notice, and the discovery of the tiny piece of wood that was the little finger of the Infant Jesus.

By the time she had finished speaking it had grown quite dark outside, and the fire no longer leaped and crackled but had sunk to a furry pink-and-gray glow. Moses was in a profound slumber and the bishop himself sat silent and motionless, pondering what he had heard.

"Do you have the Child's finger with you?" he asked at last.

Without speaking, Hannah unfastened the clasp of her locket, opened it, and passed it to him. Moses's sleep was disturbed by the movement and he looked up, gave her a deeply offended stare, then shifted his weight onto her right leg. Gradually, she felt the blood supply returning while her other foot began to go numb instead.

The bishop took out the tiny fragment of wood, placed it in the palm of his hand, and regarded it lovingly for several minutes. Then he carefully replaced the finger and put the locket down on the table between them.

Abruptly he stood up, took a well-thumbed Bible from the bookcase, and rapidly found the page he wanted. "Are you familiar with St. Matthew's gospel?"

"I'm afraid not," replied Hannah apologetically. "I . . . we . . . don't really go to church, and I . . . I don't know that I believe in God!" She blushed, but the bishop seemed quite unconcerned by this announcement. He put the Bible in her hands and pointed to a place on the page. "I wonder if you would mind reading those verses."

Hannah looked surprised but did as she was told.

"'For I was an hungred, and ye gave me meat: thirsty, and ye gave me drink: I was a stranger, and ye took me in: Naked, and ye clothed me: I was sick, and ye visited me: I was in prison, and ye came unto me.'"

She looked up at him, and he pointed to another sentence, a few lines down the page.

"'Verily I say unto you, Inasmuch as ye have done it unto one of the least of these my brethren, ye have done it unto me.'"

"I don't understand," said Hannah in bewilderment. "What has all this got to do with me?"

But the bishop didn't seem to hear. He was pacing up and down and looking agitated, muttering something to himself. After a few moments he turned to face her. "One thing seems quite plain to me, which is that while that little piece of wood is in your possession, you may be in danger. I would feel happier if you let me look after it."

"I'm afraid I can't do that," said Hannah, shaking her head unhappily. "You see, I think I've been sort of entrusted with it."

"Ah yes," murmured the bishop. "Quite so." He sighed. "Very well," he said at last. "It is a risk, but I fear it is a risk that I have no right to take from you. Tell me, before all this happened, what would you say was your ambition?"

Hannah considered this abrupt change of subject with surprise. "Well, to be an artist I guess. A portrait artist."

"Anything else?"

"I want to be thin and not have bad skin anymore and be good at math!" This came out in a rush.

"Ah! And now?"

"Now I just want to find the missing baby," Hannah replied sadly.

They were both silent for some moments while

the bishop again seemed lost in his own thoughts. Then he recollected himself and sat up, brisk and practical.

"Then that is that," he said, as though they had just come to a joint decision. "You will need help, and I will do my utmost to obtain it for you. And now you must be off. Your parents will be concerned."

"You mean you aren't going to tell me to go home and forget all about it?" Hannah was relieved and startled all at once. Was this the behavior of a responsible adult?

"Good heavens, no! On whose authority could I give such an instruction?"

Hannah privately thought that if a bishop didn't have sufficient authority to instruct her, probably no one would.

"Besides, if I were to tell you to go home and forget all about it, what would you do? Could you stop wondering? Could you forget what you've seen?"

"No." And suddenly she knew that what he said was true. The small statues had become part of her life. It was a simple and irreversible fact.

The bishop rose from his chair and pressed a bell underneath the mantelpiece. A few seconds later a face appeared at the door. The jaw dropped at the sight of Hannah, and she recognized the young man who had told her to come back tomorrow between the hours of ten and four.

"Would you ask Len to bring the car around please, Simon? Miss Price would like a ride home."

The man shut his mouth with an affronted snap and disappeared.

Soon there was a knock at the door and Hannah found herself saying good-bye to her host, who held her hand between both of his in a firm grasp, his face troubled.

"Don't worry," she said in an attempt to reassure him. "I can look after myself."

"Oh no you can't," he replied seriously. "No one can do that. But you can be vigilant, and you must."

Then Hannah got into the waiting car and the bishop returned to his study and remained there, alone in the darkness, for a long time.

Soon Hannah was in her street, which looked comfortingly ordinary at the end of a day that had been strange and confusing. Old Mr. Bryer's TV flickered companionably behind his net curtain, the two children from next door were coming back from taking their puppy for a walk, a tall man wearing a badly fitting suit with trousers far too short for him and carrying a clipboard was going from house to house, doing some kind of survey probably, and her mother was standing at the window, watching anxiously for her.

CHAPTER EIGHTEEN

FACING FACTS

"WHAT THIS PROVES is that somebody knows you've got the finger and is trying to get a message to someone else, to tell them you've got it. It still doesn't tell us how they knew in the first place."

They were standing beside the playground fence at lunchtime, a little way apart from the others so that Hannah could tell Sam about the locket without being overheard. He was holding the copy of the cooking club notice and frowning.

"It doesn't tell us why they want it, either," she replied, "and without knowing why they stole the statue in the first place, I don't see how we're going to find out."

"I suppose we're assuming it got broken by accident, are we?"

"Well, what else? Why would anyone break it deliberately?"

He turned his head to one side, thoughtfully biting his lip. "I did a search on the internet last night."

"What for?"

"I tried typing in 'devil worship.'"

"And?"

He shrugged. "Load of junk mostly. Secret signs and symbols and stuff like that."

"Nothing useful then?"

"N . . . no. Not really."

She looked at him curiously. For the first time since she'd known him, he seemed lost—unsure of himself—as though he'd wandered into a strange city without a map.

"There was one thing, though," he said at last. "Two, really."

"Go on."

"If you want to harm someone, you can take something from them—a few nail clippings or a bit of hair or something—and use whatever it is to make them ill, or even make them die if you're a really powerful witch."

"So? What's the point of breaking off part of the statue? They've already got the whole thing. They can harm that as much as they like."

"It seems like spells can work two ways. Backward and forward."

"What do you mean?"

He looked uncomfortable. "That's the other thing. I may have gotten this wrong, but it looks as though if you put a curse on someone and hurt them, and somebody else has got part of them like hair or nail clippings or . . . or . . ."

"Or a finger?"

"Well . . . "

"That somebody else could be harmed too. Is that what you mean?"

"Like I said, I could have got it wrong."

"But the statue's not real. It's only made of wood."

For some reason, Miss Murdoch's words came back to her just then. "It is said that when an oak tree is felled, it screams, like a person!"

She shivered, then shook her head impatiently. "You're forgetting something."

"What?"

"I found the finger by accident. No one gave it to me. In fact we know for a fact they're trying to get it back."

"Yes. Unless . . . "

"Unless what?"

"Unless it found you."

She stared at him. "I thought you didn't believe all that stuff about magic and evil and everything!"

He frowned. "Let me have another look at that locket, will you?"

She looked at him in surprise but unclasped it and handed it over. He regarded it in silence for a few moments; then his attention seemed to be caught by something on the far side of the playground.

"What are they staring at?" he demanded.

She followed his glance and saw Tabitha with a small group of friends, apparently observing them from a distance. She shrugged and turned back, feeling vaguely disturbed.

He gave her back the locket, then stared once more at the cooking club notice. Irritably he crumpled the sheet of paper into a tight ball and banged his fist into the palm of the other hand. "We're just wasting our time! There's no point trying to work out why whoever it is stole the statue, broke it, then wrote some daft notice and stuck it on the board. We'll never solve it that way!"

"How, then?"

He put his head to one side and looked at her. "You've said it!"

"What?"

"How! That's what we've got to find out. Not why, but how."

"But we know how. There were loads of people around at the end of the evening service and someone took advantage of the crowd to pick up the statue. It's easily small enough to be hidden in a bag or under a coat. Anyone could have done it. In any case, they realized it was missing after they'd all gone and the staff were closing up the cathedral."

"How do you know that?"

"One of the people who works there told me. I went on Saturday afternoon to do some sketching. He recognized me because he was there when I drew the statues the day before the theft. Remember?"

Sam nodded. His eyes glittered. "And he told the police about you! Listen! Suppose they're wrong? What if it's an inside job?"

"Are you crazy? Those people work for the cathedral! They don't get paid for it—they do it out of love! What on earth would they want to steal that little statue for?"

"Who cares? Like I said, we've got to find out how, not why. Anyone working inside the place is bound to have a much better chance of stealing something from it than an outsider. It's the same anywhere. If money's missing from a store register, who do you suspect? The customer or the person who works at the store?"

"All right, all right." She sighed. "But we're not talking about stores. We're talking about . . ." How could she explain to him about the chaplain? The idea of him being responsible for the theft was so ridiculous! "Anyway, the police have already talked to the cathedral staff."

"But they've only got their word about when the statue was stolen. What if that chaplain was lying?"

"Look! He's just not the lying type. Okay? If you met him, you'd know that."

"Give me a chance then."

"How?"

"Will he be there after school?"

Hannah shook her head wearily. "Oh, all right. It'll be a waste of time, though."

"Amateur sleuths, eh?" The chaplain regarded them fondly and wagged his head. "Used to be keen on all that kind of thing when I was a boy! Remember Dick Barton?"

Hannah and Sam looked blank.

"No, no. Of course you wouldn't. Too young! Ah well, what can I do for you? The police had me go over it all pretty thoroughly, I can tell you. I don't suppose there's anything they missed, but go ahead."

Hannah swallowed hard. This was going to be tricky. Somehow they had to find out exactly what had happened after the evening service on Saturday, October twenty-ninth, without seeming to accuse the cathedral staff in general and the man in front of them in particular. She glanced nervously at Sam, willing him to be tactful.

"Perhaps I can help by filling in a few details," suggested the chaplain. "Evensong was sung as usual, at four thirty. It's the same every day except Sunday, when it's at three fifteen. The service lasts about forty minutes. Normally we wait till the congregation has gone, then check to see nothing's been left behind, lock up, and go home. But that afternoon, when I was doing a final look around, I noticed that the statue was missing."

"What time would that have been?" asked Sam, poising a pencil over a notepad in an impressive imitation of an eager young detective.

"Well, as I said, the service lasted about forty minutes, so it would have been over by, say, ten past five. It usually takes us another forty minutes to lock up, and I noticed the statue was missing just before we were about to do that, so . . . it would have been about ten to six. I think that's what I told the police. Not that it seems to make much difference. That was only when I noticed it was gone. The theft must have taken place right at the end of the service, when the people were leaving. Five fifteen or thereabouts."

"Was it just you who noticed?" asked Hannah.

"I was the first, then I told Tom Evans, one of the other chaplains. We asked Mrs. Crawford if she'd moved it for some reason, and that was when we noticed she wasn't well."

"Mrs. Crawford?" Sam and Hannah spoke simultaneously.

"That's right. There were just the three of us on duty that day." He looked puzzled. "What's the matter?"

"There's a Mrs. Crawford who teaches history at our school," Hannah explained. "She was taken ill sometime that weekend. Could it have been the same person?"

"As a matter of fact, I believe I do recall her telling me she was a history teacher. She just helps out here on Saturdays and Sundays."

Sam and Hannah glanced at each other. Was this the connection they'd been looking for? "What did she say when you asked her about the statue?" asked Hannah.

"That was just it! She could hardly speak, poor soul! Said her face felt numb. She had it wrapped up in a scarf. As I told you before, I was all ready to call an ambulance, but she wouldn't hear of it. Said we had enough to worry about with the missing statue, and she went home. Next thing we heard, she'd been admitted to the hospital with a stroke."

"And that was what we heard on that Monday morning," said Hannah thoughtfully. "Does she live by herself, or is there a Mr. Crawford?"

"I never heard her mention her husband. She mentioned her sister once or twice though. Beatrice I think she's called. I've a feeling they live together."

"Where's Mrs. Crawford now?" asked Sam.

"Still in the hospital, so far as I know. Were you thinking of visiting her?"

"Yes," he replied slowly. "I think we will."

"Well, give her my best wishes then. Tell her Maurice Bridges hopes she'll be better soon. And now, if you'll excuse me, I'd better lock up before anything else goes missing!"

CHAPTER NINETEEN

TABITHA'S PARTY

THERE WAS A BUZZ OF EXCITEMENT in the classroom on Wednesday morning. In ten days' time Tabitha was having a birthday party, and it seemed everyone in the class had an invitation on their desk.

"Thanks, Tabitha!" came from various chairs around the room. Tabitha smiled her mysterious smile and fluttered her black eyelashes.

"I've got nothing to wear," complained Susie at break time. "And it's going to be really chic. Sophie says they're having a live band. It must be a huge house! I guess that's why she can invite the whole class, not that there's such a big class right now, with so many kids sick with the flu. What will you wear, Emily?"

"Not sure," replied Emily without looking up

from an essay she was checking for errors. "How about you, Hannah?"

"I'm not going," said Hannah from behind the lid of her desk.

"What? Don't be stupid, of course you are! Everybody'll be there. Sam, tell Hannah she's got to come."

"What's going on?" Sam wandered over to find out what Susie was asking him to do.

"Hannah's saying she's not coming to Tabitha's party."

"So? Why should she if she doesn't want to? I probably won't go either."

"But you've been invited?" Hannah's voice was slightly wobbly.

"Sure. We all were!"

"I wasn't," said Hannah quietly.

For a moment, Sam and Susie stared at her in astonishment.

"You must have been invited," said Susie at last. "Everybody was. Even that new girl, Jessica. I heard Tabitha telling Lisa last week. Your invitation's probably dropped on the floor or something."

"Nope. I looked."

"Then there's been a mistake. I'll go and ask Tabitha now!"

"No!" said Hannah, alarmed. "What if she didn't want to ask me?"

"That's stupid," said Sam. "Why would she leave you out? Susie's right. Your invitation's just lost."

"It might be better not to mention it though," said Emily, putting her essay in her desk and joining the little group that had gathered around Hannah. "Just in case . . . you know."

"Just in case what?" demanded Sam. "Just in case she's deliberately asked everyone except Hannah?"

But Emily only looked worried and moved away. After a few seconds Susie joined her and they began talking quietly, every so often stealing a glance in Hannah's direction.

Hannah turned away from them. "Sam," she said, "you don't think it could have anything to do with, you know, what Emily was talking about last week? When she said Tabitha had been looking in my pockets?"

He glanced over to where Tabitha was laughing and chatting with a group of look-alike girls. "You think she's behind this weird thing with the finger? You think she wrote that notice? You think she stole the statue and broke into your house?"

Hannah sighed miserably. "I suppose not. But if she didn't, why didn't she invite me to her party? I mean, I know it's not important, not really, but it does look as if she kind of hates me. Doesn't it?"

Sam looked at Hannah. Then he turned and looked back at Tabitha.

"I'll tell you something," he said at last. "I can believe in her and her friends running a coven a lot better than I can believe Millie Murdoch doing it. At least they look like a bunch of witches!"

He went back to his place and Hannah opened her desk again to search for the books she would need for the first lesson, but hardly saw what she was doing as tears of shame filled her eyes. There could be only one reason why Tabitha hadn't invited her to the party. She was ugly, and nobody liked her! She peered surreptitiously around the edge of the desk lid and saw, just as she expected, the group of black-haired, white-faced girls glancing in her direction and whispering. She felt her face burning. Then she noticed Emily. She was looking at her too. Feeling sorry for her, she thought bitterly.

Suddenly she noticed the picture she had drawn of Emily lying near the bottom of her desk. She drew it out and stared at it. On an impulse, she took out her pen and jabbed it angrily at the lovely face, over and over again until it looked as though Emily had an ugly blue rash. She stared at in grim satisfaction for a few minutes.

Then, gradually, her anger subsided and she felt guilty. Guilty and stupid. What had Emily ever done to her except try to be nice? It wasn't her fault that she was beautiful.

Slowly she tore the picture in half, balled it up, and tossed it into the wastepaper basket.

CHAPTER TWENTY

ENCOUNTER IN A VEGETABLE STORE

"SMALL CABBAGE three potatoes two carrots two apples (not Granny Smiths) one banana small frozen chicken pie four ounces cooked ham small white loaf of bread plain cookies pint of milk." Hannah dutifully read Mrs. Abbott's list back to her so she could check it before she went shopping.

"Make sure he doesn't give you old carrots—last ones were all dried out."

"Okay."

"And real milk, none of this stuff that's half water!"

With a sigh of relief, Hannah escaped and set off for the shops. She bought the pie, the ham, the bread, the cookies, and the milk from a little supermarket a short walk away, then went another fifty yards until she came to the greengrocer's.

"Small cabbage please," she said when she got to the front of the line.

"This one okay?" The man held up something the size of a football.

"Haven't you got one a bit smaller?"

"No."

"All right. Three potatoes. And two carrots. Not too big. She said the last ones were a bit dried out."

"She did, did she?" The man's voice was sarcastic and Hannah felt herself blushing.

"Two apples," she said quickly, as he weighed the carrots. "Not Granny Smiths—Coxes, please."

"No Coxes left. Only these Red Delicious." He indicated a box of wrinkled-looking red apples.

"Don't bother. She won't like those." There were now five people in the line behind her and she could sense their impatience. "And a banana."

"Just the one banana?" enquired the man heavily.

"Yes thanks."

"This one small enough, or would you like me to cut it in half for you?"

There was a small ripple of appreciation at this

humorous remark, and Hannah unzipped Mrs. Abbott's purse quickly in an attempt to get out of the store as soon as possible, causing half a dozen coins to scatter on the grimy floor. Blushing even more furiously, she bent down to pick them up.

"Excuse me," she said to the woman standing next to her. "Would you mind moving your foot? I think you're standing on my money." The brown lace-up shoe moved a fraction of an inch and Hannah retrieved the coin and stood up.

"One sixty-four."

Frantically she glanced from her hand to the purse to the floor. She hardly had anything left over from the supermarket! "Just a minute," she muttered, feeling in her pocket in case she had some change there.

The greengrocer put both hands on the counter and grimly looked prepared to wait all day if necessary. The shuffling and murmuring from behind grew louder.

"The Grapes of Wrath!"

Everyone in the shop, including Hannah, jumped at this announcement, which was delivered in a resonant voice from the doorway by a tall man inspecting a large bunch of seedless green grapes. He was holding a clipboard and wearing a suit whose trousers seemed to have been made for somebody else, as they were several inches too short. Hannah vaguely remembered seeing someone who looked like that near her house after she'd returned from visiting the bishop.

"And the fruit of the Garden of Eden!" The man looked curiously at the box of wizened red apples and then gave the assembled customers a dazzling smile. They stared at him, openmouthed, as if he had just arrived from some distant planet.

Hannah lost no time in taking advantage of the interruption. "I'll give you the rest next time," she murmured to the storekeeper, who took no notice whatsoever.

When she got outside, she found that the owner of the brown shoes had also finished her shopping and followed her out of the door. She glanced upward, taking in the plaid skirt, the large, pale face, the round glasses, and gave a start of recognition. It was the social worker! At last she had a chance to remind the woman she had seen her before.

"Hi!" began Hannah nervously. "You remember me, don't you? You were visiting the Fallons about a month ago and I was there too. It was a Saturday," she added helpfully.

"Really? I'm afraid I don't remember. I make many house calls and a month ago is a long time."

Hannah bit her lip in frustration. If only the woman had been more observant!

"I'm sorry, was there something you wanted to tell me? About Mrs. Fallon, perhaps?"

"No, nothing," muttered Hannah. "It doesn't matter."

"Perhaps I can offer you a ride somewhere?" The woman unlocked the door of a small car parked directly outside the store. "Those bags look heavy."

Hannah considered this. She wasn't supposed to accept rides from strangers, of course, but the woman was a social worker, after all. And besides, if she talked with her for a little longer she might just remember her.

But as she was about to accept, she noticed the tall man with the too-short trousers standing nearby, regarding the small car with interest.

"Dear me," he said to nobody in particular. "This car has a flat tire."

The social worker gave an angry exclamation when she looked down and saw the deflated tire. "I shall have to call the car service," she muttered, pulling her cell phone from her handbag.

She seemed to have forgotten all about Hannah.

In any case, she couldn't do anything to help, and as she picked up her shopping and began to walk back to Mrs. Abbott's, she noticed that the tall man had disappeared.

CHAPTER TWENTY-ONE

MRS. CRAWFORD

"I DON'T KNOW WHAT YOU'RE expecting to find out," complained Hannah as she and Sam turned in through the gates of the city hospital that afternoon. "Unless you think Mrs. Crawford stole the statue and then was so overcome by guilt she had a stroke and now she's going to admit it and hand herself over to the police."

"She might have seen something. Something suspicious. For all we know, that could've been what made her ill."

"Then the police will have asked her already."

"That chaplain in the cathedral said she couldn't talk properly. They probably haven't been able to get anything out of her."

"Then what are we doing here? If she couldn't

talk to them, she won't be able to talk to us either!"

"She could be better by now. People recover from strokes."

"Well what are we going to ask her? Assuming she can understand us, that is."

But now they had arrived at Reception and Sam was talking to a woman behind a desk.

"Willow Ward, straight down the corridor, right at the end, take the elevator down one, turn left, go through a set of double doors, and it's on your right," she said without looking up from the card she was filling in.

After two wrong turns they found it.

"Can I help you?" asked a harassed-looking nurse at the entrance to the ward.

"We've come to see Mrs. Crawford," said Sam.

"Are you relatives?"

"No," said Hannah.

"Yes," said Sam. "She's my auntie. My mom's sister. Mom would have come herself, but she's got to visit my dad, so I said I'd come instead. I hope Auntie's not . . . any worse?" This was said with a faint wobble of the lower lip.

"Oh dear," said the nurse, looking worried. "I'm surprised your mother sent you. We told her over the phone that her sister's condition had deteriorated. It seems to be a much more severe stroke than we thought at first. You could sit with her for a few moments and just chat, but I don't think you'll get much response." She led them to a small private room and opened the door. Then she left.

Mrs. Crawford was lying on her back, but her eyes were open.

Hannah sat on a chair beside the bed and took the teacher's hand. It felt dry and cold. "Mrs. Crawford," she said, "it's Hannah Price. And Sam Fallon. We've come to see you."

The eyes seemed to give a flicker of recognition and the lips moved very slightly, but no sound came out.

"Can you hear me, Mrs. Crawford? If you can, squeeze my hand."

She thought she felt the faintest possible answering pressure, but she couldn't be sure. It could have been just her imagination.

"Look, there's no point staying here," said Sam. "She can't hear us, and even if she could, she's not going to be able to tell us anything."

"Okay." Hannah got to her feet.

"How was she?" asked the nurse when they were out of the room.

"You were right," said Sam. "She didn't know

who we were." Which was just as well, he reflected, since he was pretty certain a conscious Mrs. Crawford wouldn't have wanted him for a nephew.

"I'm afraid there's been very little change since she was brought in last month," said the nurse. "I'm surprised. I'd have expected some sort of recovery by now, especially as the ambulance men said she could just about make herself understood when they picked her up."

"Did she call the ambulance herself?" asked Sam.

"I can't tell you that. I assume it was her sister though. Miss Arnold. She's been in to see her once or twice, but I don't think she came with her when she was admitted. I was on duty that evening and I remember it because it was such a busy time for a new admission. We were trying to serve the evening meal."

Sam glanced around the ward. Then he frowned. "But a meal's being served now."

"That's right. Five thirty. I must get going." She glanced at her watch and started to move away.

"You mean she was brought in at five thirty?"

"About then, yes."

"Don't you keep records of things like that?" The nurse gave him a strange look but crossed to the desk and looked through some notes. "Five twenty-two, Saturday, October the twenty-ninth," she told them, returning. "Wait a minute though!" She looked at Sam. "Why were you asking all those questions about Mrs. Crawford's sister? She's your mother, isn't she?"

"My mom's got two sisters," said Sam. "This other one . . . they don't talk, see. Haven't spoken in years." He shook his head sorrowfully and made a swift exit from the ward, pulling Hannah with him.

"What was all that about?" asked Hannah when they were in the elevator.

"Don't you see? That man in the cathedral told us he'd asked Mrs. Crawford about the statue when they realized it was missing. That was *after* the service. Just before they were about to lock up. About ten to six, he said. At ten to six, she'd already been in hospital for nearly half an hour!"

She stared at him. "He might have made a mistake and been confused about the times."

"He couldn't have been wrong about the time of the service, though. Except for Sundays, it's always at four thirty and it lasts forty minutes. Even if they took half as long to lock up at the end, that still brings the time to five thirty. That's eight minutes after she was brought in here!"

"But that means the chaplain wasn't telling the truth."

"Exactly! And you said he wasn't the lying type!" He couldn't keep the triumph out of his voice.

"I can't believe it," she said slowly.

"Well, you'll have to. There's no other explanation. He had the opportunity to steal the statue, and now we know he's trying to hide the truth about what happened. What more proof do you want?"

"Motive?"

He shrugged. "These religious types are weird. Who knows what he planned to do with it?"

Again Miss Murdoch's words came back to her.

"Magic and miracles . . . witches have always been persecuted but priests respected!"

A thought struck her. "Miss Murdoch knew—knows Mrs. Crawford, doesn't she?"

"I don't know. Probably."

"I mean, I've seen them talking together outside the staff room."

"So?"

"She might know about her working in the cathedral."

"Yes?" He started to look interested.

"And she could even have been with her at home when she had the stroke."

"Go on."

"Listen! Suppose Miss Murdoch wanted to steal the statue. All she'd have to do would be to make sure Mrs. Crawford was safely out of the way when she was supposed to be on duty in the cathedral, go there herself instead, put on one of those black robes they all wear, and pretend to be her!"

"But the man, chaplain, whatever, he would know it wasn't Mrs. Crawford. He's seen her before."

"Don't you remember what he said? She had a scarf around her face and she couldn't talk properly! He thought it was because she'd had a stroke, but it would have been a perfect way for Millie Murdoch to disguise herself, and afterward no one would suspect anything because the hospital would confirm it."

He whistled. "Makes sense, sort of. Wait a minute though. This theft must have been thought of in advance, even if it wasn't planned exactly. How would Millie know she was going to have a stroke? Or did she just put a spell on her?" A note of skepticism crept into his voice.

"All right! You think of a better theory then!"

"Okay, okay. Keep calm. It's good, I admit. So what do we do now? Tell the police the times don't add up?"

"I guess so."

"Then what? They've got no evidence against Millie, nor against anyone else for that matter. Can you see them taking us seriously?"

Hannah thought of Detective Sergeant Bean. Then she thought of Detective Constable Clutterbuck and suddenly felt depressed. "You're right. There's nothing we can do. Not yet."

CHAPTER TWENTY-TWO

LOST IN THE FOG

FOR THE NEXT WEEK Hannah had little time to spare for anything except her painting and some school-work. Sam was beginning to get bored with sitting still for so long, but fortunately she could now get on with some of the work without him being there, and she was enjoying seeing the results of painting in this new way.

The national newspapers had long ago stopped mentioning the theft from the cathedral and were full of the flu epidemic, which was becoming more serious every day, with buses and trains and hospitals all short staffed and many schools closed. Manningham was still open, but quite a few of the teachers were absent, their lessons either canceled or covered by colleagues who found themselves taking classes that got smaller each day as more students became ill. Even Miss Murdoch was away, which took Hannah's mind off her suspicions for the time being.

In the end, Tabitha's party never took place, partly because there were so few people left to go, but also because most parents were afraid of letting their children go where there were others who might infect them. Tabitha herself seemed to avoid Hannah, but mostly she was too preoccupied to mind.

A week before the entry date Hannah completed Sam's portrait. It was the most ambitious thing she had ever done. She was still not entirely satisfied with it, and she wondered if the skin tones were just slightly too dark, but as she stood back and tried to observe it critically and objectively, Sam looked back at her from the canvas; a sidelong glance, faintly arrogant, mocking, humorous. She smiled back at his image. Yes, it was Sam all right, the Sam she knew so well!

Miss Beamish inspected it carefully and then was silent for a little while.

"The thing is, Hannah," she said at last, "anyone can learn the technique of oil painting, given time and application, but to bring the essence of a person to life, like you have done with Sam, well, that's a very rare gift indeed. I knew we were right to choose you!"

Sam himself was less complimentary. "What's that stupid grin on my face?" he demanded.

"That's your own stupid grin! Don't blame me. I only paint what I see."

Monday was the last day for Hannah to see the portrait before it was sent to London to be judged, and as soon as school was over she gathered up her books before making her way to the art room for one last look. But while she was still standing at her desk she heard the sound of running footsteps, and Susie burst in.

"Hannah! Come quick!" Susie's voice was urgent and frightened. "Miss Beamish told me to get you! It's your painting! Someone's scribbled all over it!"

Hannah felt a cold hand grip her stomach. She tried to run, but her legs felt as though they were made of lead. Somewhere at the back of her mind was the realization that she'd been expecting something like this to happen—it was as if she were watching a repeat of a film she'd seen before.

When they reached the art room her breath was caught by an overpowering smell of turpentine.

Miss Beamish was standing in front of an easel with a rag in her hand. Next to her was Mr. Cristanthi, and as Hannah approached, they stood back to reveal the portrait. She stopped abruptly, and her heart seemed to stop with her.

For a second she thought it was a joke. Someone had found the Halloween mask and stuck it on the painting! But it wasn't a joke. Deep frown lines scored the forehead; the eyes had been crudely altered so that the pupils converged on the nose in a wicked leer; the line of the mouth was now a cruel slash, turned down at the corners, with two long canines pointing down from the top lip, blood dripping to the edge of the canvas. Sam was no longer the friend she knew. He had become a vampire.

"Who—who did this?" she whispered at last.

"I'm afraid I can't tell you that," said Miss Beamish sadly. "All I can say is that it wasn't like this when I left the room half an hour ago." Here her voice shook a little and she turned to Hannah. "I'm so sorry, so very sorry—I should have kept a close watch on it, but I never expected that anyone would do a thing like this!"

"Did you see anything?" Hannah turned to Mr. Cristanthi.

He shook his head with a baffled frown. "I was

talking to Miss Beamish in the staff room. We were discussing the introduction of an art history club. She asked me if I'd like to see the portrait before it was sent away, and of course I said yes! We came down here, and this is what we found. Can you think of anyone who would want to do this to you, or to Sam, perhaps?"

Hannah thought of Tabitha. Would she? Given her behavior recently, it seemed quite possible, but Hannah couldn't think why she would do something so awful. "I don't know," she said slowly. "I don't suppose there are any signs . . . ?" She looked vaguely at the floor, half hoping whoever it was might have dropped something incriminating.

"I'll have a look outside," offered Mr. Cristanthi.

As he left the room, Miss Beamish recovered herself and began rubbing at the new paint with a turpentine-soaked rag. Hannah watched, trembling in agitation.

A few moments later Mr. Cristanthi reappeared, shaking his head. "No sign of anything, I'm afraid. How's the cleanup job going?" He moved to the easel and seemed to be inspecting both it and the portrait closely, then backed off to view the painting from a distance.

"Nearly back to normal," said Miss Beamish

with relief. "Thank goodness we found it when we did. By tomorrow some of the paint would have been so dry we wouldn't have been able to get it off without ruining the whole picture."

"Wait a minute!" said Hannah. "What's that?"

"What's what?"

"That piece of paper. Look." She stepped forward and pointed to something that was lodged between the canvas and the easel, very slightly protruding above the top.

"Oh! Why didn't we notice that before?" Miss Beamish reached up and drew out a slip of paper, roughly folded. She stared at it in astonishment, then handed it to Hannah. "It's got your name on it!"

Hannah took it from her and looked at the teacher briefly before unfolding the paper.

I KNOW WHO DID THIS. MEET ME AT MY HOUSE AS SOON AS POSSIBLE. SAM

"What is it?" asked Miss Beamish.

"Nothing," she said hastily. "Just an old note. I've got to go now. Is it okay to leave the painting with you?"

"Don't worry, it's not going to leave my sight

until it's safely wrapped up and sent away!" replied Miss Beamish grimly.

When she got outside she noticed that a cold, thin fog had descended over the city, dimming headlights and obscuring familiar landmarks.

Even so, walking fast, it took her only twenty minutes to reach the Fallons' building. She ran up the staircase, shoes ringing on the cold stained concrete, and rang the bell. She waited. Then she rang again, for longer this time. Maybe Sam wasn't home yet? But the note had said "as soon as possible." Wouldn't Eve be there now, with the twins? She banged loudly with the knocker. Then with her fist. But no welcoming footsteps answered her knock.

She turned away from the door to think. Should she wait? Or should she walk back toward the school and hope to meet Sam on his way home? She decided to walk. Anything was better than standing still in this depressing place.

She made her way more slowly down the staircase, until she reached the concrete walkway that linked the Fallons' building to the others in the complex. The walk was littered with broken glass, rusty metal parts, empty beer cans, and blowing newspapers. She had never been here without Sam before, and noticed for the first time how alike all the buildings were; identical in fact. She turned left toward the main road but after about twenty yards was brought up short by a dead end. She must have turned too early. She retraced her steps and tried the next walkway. Another dead end. She looked back toward Sam's building, confused. Then she realized what she must have done. There were two staircases leading down from the Fallons' apartment to ground level. Somehow she had taken the wrong one and ended up at the back instead of the front.

She turned around and walked back the way she had come, this time turning right at the main walkway. When she got to the Fallons' building, she made her way to the other side, looking out for the base of the staircase she should have taken to start with. Then she noticed the number on the door of the nearest apartment. It was 512. That was odd. Sam's flat was 235. The first number just referred to the building—she knew that. Which meant that this wasn't where Sam lived after all. He was probably home now and impatiently waiting for her!

She peered into the gloom, searching for somebody she could ask, but the only sign of life was a thin gray dog sniffing at a pile of newspapers. She moved toward it, thinking that an owner might be nearby, but as she approached the dog it ran off.

She stood still, uncertain which way to turn. Sam's apartment was three buildings away, but in which direction? The fog was thicker now and she could hardly see the farther buildings, let alone read the numbers on the doors. The sound of a motorcycle engine in the distance gave her hope, and she turned her head, trying to figure out where it came from. But the fog confused her sense of direction and as she ran toward the noise, it seemed to go away.

A dull ache lurked somewhere behind her temples and she began to shiver. Thrusting her hands into her pockets she forced herself to walk quickly, to get warm. It didn't seem to make much difference which direction she took since she didn't know where she was anyway, so she set off down a walkway between two high buildings. After about fifty yards she reached a corner, and could just make out numbers on the side of the building. She had to get right up close to read them, and as she did so, her heart sank.

"800–850." She stared at the figures in disbelief. Sam's apartment must be six buildings away! But which way? For the first time, she started to panic. Her head throbbed painfully and she felt very cold.

It was dark and foggy and she was lost in a hostile, featureless place where everything looked the same. She leaned miserably against the hard concrete wall and tried to think, but even her brain felt numb with cold.

Then in the distance she saw a figure approaching slowly out of the fog, carrying two shopping bags. As the figure drew closer she saw that it belonged to an old woman, heavily bundled up against the cold and wearing a thick head scarf. Hannah forced herself away from the support of the wall and hurried toward her.

"Excuse me," she said breathlessly. "I'm looking for apartment two three five. Do you know where it is?"

The woman peered at her, cupping a hand behind her ear. "Speak up, dear."

"I said do you know where apartment two three five is? I'm lost." She raised her voice and bent her head closer to the old woman's face, which was half hidden beneath the thick scarf.

"Two three five? That's in my building. I'll take you there if you want, but you'll have to go slow on account of my legs."

"Oh, thank you!" Hannah breathed a sigh of relief. She didn't mind walking slowly, since her head now ached unbearably, but she hoped she wouldn't die of cold before they got there. She knew she should offer to carry the old lady's shopping, but just then she didn't think she could support anything more than her own weight. She felt weak and light-headed.

"Visiting a friend, are you?" enquired her companion after a minute or so.

"Yes."

"You all right, dear?" The old woman peered at her, frowning. "You don't look well."

"I'm okay." She shivered, and thought longingly of the Fallons' warm, welcoming apartment and prayed that they wouldn't be out.

They walked on in silence for a while. Hannah was hardly aware which way they were going, only concentrating on putting one foot in front of the other, trying not to fall on the littered, slippery path.

"Is it far now?" she asked at last, looking around her for the first time.

"Not far. Just beyond this next block."

"But this doesn't look right." She peered up at the tall buildings, puzzled. They seemed to be in the heart of the complex. Surely Sam's apartment was near the edge? Perhaps the old lady hadn't heard her properly.

"Are you sure this is the right building? I need two three five." She tried to speak clearly, but her teeth were chattering so much she could hardly frame the words.

"I heard you," muttered the old lady.

They had reached the end of the block. But there were no steps here, and no lights. Only a small, evil-smelling area, enclosed on three sides and containing a row of overflowing garbage cans, surrounded by a litter of plastic bottles and broken glass.

"We must have taken a wrong turn," said Hannah, frowning. "There's no way into the building from here."

"This is as far as we're going."

Hannah stared at her, not quite able to take in what she was hearing.

"But this is a dead end. There's no way out!"

"That's right." The old woman's voice was flat and harsh. "There's no way out now."

A dull panic filled her brain. It seemed to mix with the foul smell that seeped from the overflowing garbage cans, making her sick and dizzy. She had to get out of this horrible place, away from this strange old woman. Slowly she backed away, then turned and tried to run.

That was when she saw the second figure. It stood at the entrance to the area, and as she watched, it began to walk toward her.

Then several things seemed to happen at once. The noise of an engine broke into the silence and she was aware of a bright light, coming closer, and now it resolved itself into the twin beams of a pair of headlights, dazzling her so that she had to close her eyes against the glare. She could hear angry voices, then running footsteps, but both seemed to come from a long way off now and she couldn't tell whether it was she or they who were receding, slipping away. She felt strangely weightless.

Then somebody took her hand. The grasp had a strength that seemed to travel through her like warm, sweet water, reviving her frozen limbs and allowing her to be led away.

CHAPTER TWENTY-THREE

RIDE IN A STRANGE CAR

THE EXPLOSION SOUNDED as if it came from an exhaust pipe. Hannah opened her eyes and looked around her in bewilderment. She was sitting in the passenger seat of what appeared to be a very old, battered car, beside a man who was frowning perplexedly at the control panel and scratching his head.

"We don't seem to be going anywhere," he remarked.

"Who are you?" she demanded in alarm. "And what am I doing here?" She searched for the door handle.

"Please don't get out," said the man. "You're much safer in here, you know."

She peered through the steamed-up window at

the tall buildings of the apartment complex looming in the fog, and shivered. No, she couldn't go
back there! But equally, she couldn't accept a ride
from a strange man, and as she turned back to the
driver she saw that he was a very strange man
indeed. His arms and legs seemed far too long for
the little car; his knees were hunched uncomfortably beneath the steering wheel and his ankles
showed a gap of at least a foot between his shoes
and the bottoms of his trousers. Something stirred
in her memory. She had seen this man before. He
had been in the greengrocer's while she was shopping for Mrs. Abbott, and before that, outside her
house doing some kind of survey with a clipboard.
Was that what he'd been doing at Sam's complex?
A survey?

She shook her head to try to clear it, then regretted it as it throbbed with pain.

"Could you just take me to somewhere I can call
a taxi?" she asked weakly.

"Certainly not. How do we know who's going to
be driving it? And by the way, you'd better hang on
to that when we go around corners." He indicated a
piece of string attached to the inside door handle.

Illogically, she found the instruction vaguely
reassuring. If this was an attempt at abduction, it

was a pretty incompetent one.

She closed her eyes, resigned now to whatever fate had in store. She felt far too helpless to resist. All she wanted to do was drift off into sleep.

But she soon discovered that there was absolutely no chance of this. The man turned the key in the ignition, and after a few seconds of chugging and wheezing the small car gave vent to another deafening explosion, then shot forward like the cork from a champagne bottle before the brake was applied with such violence that the two of them were nearly projected through the windshield.

"Sorry!" said the driver cheerfully. "Better try again."

After more wheezing from the motor and grinding from the gearbox the car began to edge its way slowly and erratically out of the housing complex and onto the main road, where it abruptly and unexpectedly pulled straight out into the flow of rush-hour traffic. The tall man drove like an inexperienced rider trying to control a nervous and excitable horse. Every now and again the vehicle protested with more grinding and explosions.

"What time is it?" she shouted above the noise.

He took both hands off the wheel to consult his

watch, and the car headed determinedly for the sidewalk.

"Watch out!" she cried, as he turned the wheel violently and they made straight for a lamppost.

"Five o'clock!" he yelled above the angry blare of horns that was becoming a familiar accompaniment to their journey.

Five o'clock! Her parents would be wondering what had happened to her.

"Are you sure?" Hannah immediately regretted this question as the watch was again consulted and the little car swerved into the path of an oncoming bus.

"Quite sure!" replied the man, in cheerful unconcern for the havoc he was causing. He confidently drove through a red light.

"That light was red! Didn't you notice?" shouted Hannah desperately, beginning to wonder if she had escaped danger by abduction only to die in a car crash.

"Was it?" The man turned around interestedly in his seat to see if she was right and Hannah found herself staring into the horrified face of a van driver, inches away from her own. She closed her eyes. When she opened them again she saw to her enormous relief that they were within half a mile of home, and after another five minutes, any of which she felt might be her last, they shuddered to a halt outside her house.

"Thank you," she said faintly.

"Don't mention it," replied the man. "Sorry if my driving alarmed you. I'm new to it you see, but I'm hoping to get the hang of it soon. Now, before you go, let me give you my card." He reached into the pocket of his ill-fitting trousers, withdrew a rather bent business card, and handed it to her. "Don't hesitate to get in touch if you need me," he said. "Anytime!"

Hannah thanked him again, got shakily out of the car, and watched him drive off with a final, shattering explosion from the exhaust pipe. As he went, she tried to remember if she'd ever told him where she lived. She didn't think so, but she supposed she must have or he wouldn't have been able to find her house so easily. She peered at the card he'd given her, which bore the words:

GABRIEL JONES (ARCH.)

PRACTICAL ASSISTANCE OFFERED IN ALL AREAS.

NO JOB TOO GREAT.

She turned over the card and found an unlikely-looking telephone number containing fourteen digits, including a great many threes and sevens. It was nothing like any number she'd ever seen. She wondered vaguely what "Arch." stood for. Architect? Archaeologist? But Mr. Jones had looked far too shabby for an architect, and why would an archaeologist be doing house-to-house surveys with a clipboard? Her brain simply couldn't cope with any more puzzles tonight.

Her head was now aching unbearably, and her throat felt as if she had swallowed a bunch of razor blades. She wearily climbed the steps to the front door, found her key, and let herself in.

"Hannah! We've been so worried! Where on earth have you been?"

But Mrs. Price never got an answer to this question because her daughter had collapsed in a dead faint.

CHAPTER TWENTY-FOUR

HANNAH'S SICKNESS

HANNAH'S MEMORY of the next ten days was patchy and indistinct. She still seemed to be surrounded by a thick fog. Every so often a face would loom out of the fog, but then it would disappear again as she drifted off into a troubled, nightmarish sleep.

One dream haunted her persistently. She was lying on the floor just outside a small room whose door stood open to reveal a single flickering candle that threw enormous dancing shadows on the walls and ceiling. She could make out two hooded figures standing near, but they weren't looking at her; instead they gazed intently at some object just out of her sight. Desperately she tried to turn her head so that she could see this object, but her body was stiff and leaden, and she was powerless to move it. She tried to speak, but no sound came. Then she would wake briefly before sliding off again into unconsciousness.

At times her hands and feet felt like solid blocks of ice; at other times she thought the bedclothes must be on fire, they were so hot and painful to touch. Her head seemed to be filled with sand, which shifted whenever she moved, and there was more sand in her throat, scratching and scraping against it at each swallow.

These were the darkest days of winter, when all the world seemed to be waiting for something.

Then one day Hannah opened her eyes and found that the fog had lifted and the sand was gone. A strange, yellowish light bathed the room.

Slowly and painfully she sat up in bed and peered out the window to see a scene that looked like a black-and-white photograph. The familiar garden was transformed by a blanket of snow.

"Feeling better?" Her mother was standing in the doorway, smiling, but her voice was unsteady. She crossed the room and sat down on the bed.

Hannah noticed that she looked pale and tired.

She laid a hand on her daughter's forehead. "Good! Your temperature's down at last. We were worried you might not be well again in time for Christmas. You gave us such a scare! Dr. Fraser said it was one of the worst cases he'd ever seen. He wanted to put you in the hospital, but then the snow came and the roads were all blocked, so we kept you here, thank goodness!"

"The worst cases of what?"

"Flu, of course! Your father's had it too, but not nearly so badly as you. We began to wonder—" She stopped, unable to go on.

"What did you begin to wonder, Mom?"

"If it might have affected your brain," whispered her mother. "You said such strange things sometimes, muttering and shouting out. It looked as though you were trying to see something that wasn't there!" She pulled herself together with an effort. "Anyway, you seem a lot better now. Hungry?"

"Starving!"

"I'll get you some soup."

When she came back with the tray, she had a letter in her hand. "This arrived for you the day before yesterday. We didn't open it. Dad thought we'd better wait till you were well."

Hannah opened the envelope and took out a

folded sheet of paper. It had the A.com.o.data logo at the top.

"Dear Hannah," said the letter.

We are delighted to inform you that the judges of our Schools Portrait Contest have unanimously awarded you first prize, for your portrait: Sam Fallon. This means, as you know, that Manningham School will receive two thousand pounds' worth of computer equipment of their choice, for which we will provide expert advice as part of the award, and you will receive an individual prize of three hundred pounds for yourself, to be spent on art materials. We would like to offer you our congratulations on this splendid achievement and look forward to following your future career with great interest.

Hannah leaned back heavily on the pillows. The sand had suddenly reappeared in her head and was shifting about alarmingly.

"What is it?" asked Mom anxiously. "It's not bad news is it? Oh, I told your father we should have read it first!"

"It's okay, it's not bad news. In fact it's rather good news!" She handed the letter to her mother, who scanned it rapidly. Her expression changed from worried, to baffled, to radiant.

"Hannah, that's wonderful!" she said. "What a marvelous Christmas present for you! Three hundred pounds! Wait till Dad gets home! We're going to celebrate this evening!"

Hannah lay back and smiled contentedly. She knew that quite soon she was going to be as excited about the prize as her mother, but just now she couldn't handle it all. Soon she would have some soup.

But within a minute she had fallen into a deep, dreamless sleep.

At ten o'clock the next morning there was a ring at the door and a few moments later her mother appeared. "Visitor for you!" she said, as Sam walked into the room bearing an enormous, slightly over-ripe bunch of bananas.

"Brought you some fruit," he announced unnecessarily. "Hey! Good news about the contest! I called last night to see how you were and your mother told me. Mom sends her love and says she hopes you're feeling better. She wants to know if she can have the picture to hang in our apartment. She can see herself dusting it already."

Hannah laughed. "Did you tell your dad?"

"Told him yesterday."

"What did he say?"

"He said, 'Gawd Almighty! Why would anybody want to paint a picture of your ugly mug, son?' You could tell he was pleased, though. Of course, I don't suppose they'd have given it first prize if it'd been just anyone's picture," he said modestly.

She smiled; then her face clouded over. "I've been trying to remember what happened after I left school that day."

"The day you got sick? Didn't you go straight home?"

She shook her head. "I'd been trying to find your apartment. You left me a note telling me to meet you there. You said you knew who'd scribbled on the portrait."

"Are you serious?"

She nodded.

"I never left you any note," he said slowly. "I didn't know anything about the portrait till Miss Beamish told me about it the next day. In any case, we were all out, visiting my dad."

"That's what I was afraid of." She bit her lip. "I got lost, you see, trying to find where you lived. All those buildings look so alike. Then I met this old lady and she said she'd take me there. But she didn't. She led me to a place where there were just garbage cans and trash everywhere, and then she told me that was as far as we were going!"

"Was she crazy?"

"I don't think so," Hannah said slowly. "I think she meant to take me there, because there was someone else there too. When I tried to run off, this other person was blocking the way." She shivered at the recollection.

"What did they want?"

"I don't know. Or maybe I just can't remember. I was sick, I realize that now. The flu must have already got to me. The next thing I knew, I was in a strange car with this weird guy."

"What?"

"I saw him in the greengrocer's."

"Greengrocer's?" He stared at her. "There's no greengrocer's anywhere near those blocks!"

"Not then, about a week before. He was looking at the fruit. And he'd been outside our house a few days earlier, doing some kind of survey I think."

Sam shook his head impatiently. "Never mind about fruit and surveys. You got in a car with him?" His eyes were wide in horror.

"I don't remember getting in. I was just there, suddenly. Like I told you, I was sick," she said defensively.

"Where's the locket?" he demanded abruptly.

She gasped. Until that moment she had forgotten all about the locket. She stared at him, in the horrible realization that her illness must have robbed her of more than one memory.

But Sam had already found it on her bedside table and was turning it over thoughtfully.

"Give it to me!" She snatched it from him, and her shaking hands began to open it.

"Don't worry," he said calmly. "It's empty." He reached inside his pocket and withdrew a matchbox. Pushing it open, he took out the fragment of finger and held it out to her.

"I . . . don't understand," she whispered, as relief flooded her brain and made her weak. "How long have you had it?"

"Since that day in the playground when I asked you to let me have a look at it." He grinned. "I distracted you by telling you Tabitha was watching us. Then when you turned away, I took the finger out."

"Why?" she demanded.

"I thought that while you had it, you were a sort of target. I figured if I took it away, they might leave you alone. I guess I was wrong." He frowned.

She turned away from him so that he couldn't

see the tears that suddenly sprang into her eyes. "At least I've still got it, thanks to you," she said huskily.

He looked at her thoughtfully. "Whoever wrote that note meant you to come to my apartment. They couldn't have known you'd get lost, but they would have been looking for you."

"And they found me." Her voice trembled.

They both considered this in silence for a few moments. Then Sam spoke.

"We have to assume it was the finger they wanted, don't we?"

"I guess so."

"You think they wanted it so it could be joined to the rest of the statue? To make it . . . complete?"

"Why else?" She sniffed.

"To get it away from you?"

"What?"

"I think someone's scared of you, Hannah Price."

She looked at him blankly, astonishment drying her tears. "Scared of me? You're crazy! What have I ever done in my whole life to make anyone scared of me? People laugh at me because I've got bad skin and I'm overweight, but scared? No, Sam, this must be about something that hasn't got anything to do with me at all, but I've kind of accidentally got mixed up in it. Maybe I was just in the wrong place at the wrong time," she finished up unhappily.

"Or maybe in the right place at the right time."

"What do you mean?"

Again he was quiet for a little while, as though arranging his thoughts. Then he spoke. "Remember when the statue was first stolen and you asked me who could have done it and I said it might have been someone who just got a kick out of trashing things? Like a computer hacker?"

"Yes."

"The thing is, computers are always crashing for some reason or other. Usually it's just the fault of the person using it, accidentally giving it a command it doesn't recognize, or trying to use a program that isn't compatible with the hardware. There's nothing wrong with the computer. There's nothing wrong with the software. They just don't work together. They were never designed to."

"What's all this got to do with computers?"

"Just wait a minute. I'm getting there. What I'm trying to say, I think, is that a computer's a really complicated, powerful bit of equipment, but it has to be used in the right way, with the right program. Now take those wooden statues. Everyone in this city knows that the reason we're overrun with tourists every summer, and for most of the rest of the year as well, isn't because this is such a wonderful city, which it isn't, or because it's such a great cathedral, which it is. It's because of those statues. Once, hundreds of years ago, they could cure the sick, and ever since, people have been coming just on the off chance they still could."

"But there haven't been any convincing stories of healing for centuries!"

"I'm coming to that. Supposing, just supposing that when you did that drawing, you somehow made the right connection happen. Something that made it all work again. Like you were . . . compatible."

"I can't believe I'm hearing this, Sam Fallon! Even Mad Millie didn't go this far! And how do you explain the fact that we're suffering from the worst flu epidemic in living memory? Not much healing going on there, is there?"

"That's because the baby's been stolen."

His flat, matter-of-fact voice dropped the sentence into the conversation like a stone into a pond. It sank between them: a hard, undeniable fact, spreading ripples of implication that widened as they silently considered its frightening significance.

Sam took a deep breath and let it out slowly.

Then he shook his head as if ridding it of confusion and searched in his pocket. He pulled out a crumpled sheet of paper.

"This was stuck up on the notice board the day after you got ill. I would have missed it, but Mr. Cristanthi showed me. I suppose he thought we'd still be interested. It's another of those cooking club recipes. The problem is, I think this one's genuine. At least, I can't see anything suspicious in it."

She blew her nose and took the paper from him, straightening out the creases with the flat of her hand.

"Christmas Fruitcake!" it announced.

No need to make this in advance—with a microwave you can cook as late as December 24th and still serve a cake to delight your whole family!

A list of ingredients followed, with instructions to combine them in a plastic bowl.

"I've checked the things they tell you to put in with one of my mom's cookbooks," said Sam. "Seems they got it right this time. Quantities and all that. Mom's recipe used a regular oven, but apart from that it looks okay."

"Hm." She glanced at the bottom of the sheet.

"Six hundred and thirty seconds. How many minutes is that?" She screwed up her eyes and began counting on her fingers.

"Ten and a half," he said impatiently. "Does that sound about right?"

"Not sure. It could be. You're right, I can't see any hidden message this time. I guess they must have thought it would look funny just to put up one recipe, and added this to make the cooking club look genuine. Whoever wrote it can't spell 'normally'—it's got two *l*s, not one, but that's not exactly a crime."

He took the paper back and looked closely. " 'Which is meat, normaly.' What does that mean?"

"Ten minutes is quite a long time in a microwave. The only other thing that would take as long is meat, maybe." She shrugged. "What does it matter, anyway? It doesn't tell us anything about where to find the statue and that's all I care about."

"It's weird though—" He frowned and repeated the words softly to himself. "Which is meat. Wait a minute!"

"What?"

"*Which is meat!*"

"What are you talking about?"

"What have I just said?"

"You know what you said. You said 'which is' . . ."

"I said *'witches meet'*! Don't you understand? It's giving the time and the date of the next coven or whatever it's called! December the twenty-fourth at six thirty!"

She stared at him as light dawned. "You mean . . . but that's tomorrow! Christmas Eve!"

He nodded excitedly. "What it means is they haven't done anything to the statue yet. We've still got"—he glanced at his watch—"thirty-two hours to find it!"

"But it doesn't say where! We've no idea where to look!"

Neither of them said anything. The frustration of knowing they were so close, but still completely powerless to stop whatever mischief was being planned, struck them both dumb.

Hannah's mother appeared at the door. "I think that's enough for today, Sam," she said firmly. "Hannah needs a rest now."

"Okay." He got wearily to his feet. "I'll be seeing you."

Then he left.

After he had gone, she looked once more at the crumpled paper.

Then her heart turned to ashes as she noticed the simple words "cooking time."

So that was it. The fact that she still had the finger had made no difference in the end. At six thirty tomorrow night someone was going to burn the statue of the Child.

CHAPTER TWENTY-FIVE

CHRISTMAS EVE

December twenty-fourth began bright and intensely cold. The postman delivered the final batch of cards, and with it a large parcel. Sam's portrait. Hannah didn't unwrap it but left it just as it was, propped up against the hall table. Listlessly, she wandered into the kitchen as her father appeared carrying a shovel and the Christmas tree.

"Ground's frozen solid!" he complained. "It's taken me half an hour to get this out. Is there any coffee?"

"In the pot," replied Mom. "And don't leave that shovel there!"

Hannah sighed. The kitchen was warm and cozy and smelled deliciously of baking. In the living room cards swung gaily from their scarlet ribbon and there was a nice festive chaos everywhere. A magical time—usually.

Only this year she felt none of the magic, just a cold numbness. Something terrible was going to happen this evening, and there was nothing she could do to prevent it. Soon it would be too late.

Decorating the Christmas tree, a thing she normally loved and looked forward to, held no excitement now, but she dutifully hung the red and silver balls of glass, the dangling threads of sparkling tinsel, the tiny angels made from clay.

Because she had been ill, there had been no chance to buy presents for her parents, so there wasn't even the pleasure of giving to look forward to in the morning.

She wanted to talk with Sam. There was nothing they could do, of course, but she needed to talk to someone who knew about the turmoil that was going on inside her, and he was the only one she could confide in. She tried calling him but only got the Fallons' answering machine.

The day dragged on.

At five thirty her father sat down with the newspaper and made a start on the crossword puzzle. A special Christmas edition. Mom had a cookbook on her lap and was frowning in concentration over instructions for basting a turkey.

Hannah pretended to read a book but secretly scanned the cooking club recipe in a last, hopeless attempt to find a clue to where the statue was hidden. There was only an hour to go now. An hour till "cooking time." She felt sick with dread.

"Trough for an animal to eat in French. Six letters," announced her father, pen poised above the newspaper. "Ha! Got it! 'Manger'! He grinned triumphantly and wrote in the answer.

Hannah watched him bleakly.

"How about this one? 'Christmas treats found in spice mine.' Two words, five and four."

"Mince pies," replied his wife absently. "It's an anagram."

"What? Oh yes. Letters of 'spice mine' rearranged. Of course. That was obvious."

"Well, you didn't get it," said Mom, smiling to herself.

"I was expecting something more cryptic," he said severely.

But Hannah had stopped listening. She was staring at the paper in front of her. She was looking

at a spelling mistake. Only it wasn't a spelling mistake. It was quite deliberate. 'Normaly' spelled with
just one *l*. If you rearranged the letters, it became—
almonry.

CHAPTER TWENTY-SIX

THE ALMONRY

HER HEART WAS BEATING so fast, she couldn't think straight. How to get out of the house? How to tell Sam? She had to find a way! And she was running out of time. Then she had an inspiration.

"Just remembered!" She clapped her hand to her forehead.

"What?" asked both parents in simultaneous alarm.

"I promised Sam I'd let his mother have his portrait if it came in time for Christmas. Can I take it to her? Right now?"

They looked at each other, eyebrows raised.

"I don't see why not," said Mom. "Your father can take you in the car. You won't be long, will you?"

Hannah thought quickly. "Mrs. Fallon's going to ask me in," she said. "It would be rude not to stay for a little while, it being Christmas Eve and all that. Could you drop me off, Dad, and I'll call you when I'm ready to be picked up?"

"Oh, all right," grumbled her father. "As usual, I'm the family taxi service, but I suppose since you've been ill . . ."

"Thanks!" Hannah breathed a silent sigh of relief and ran to get her coat. She glanced at her watch. It was five forty.

The air outside was crisp and cold and came as a shock after she had been indoors so long, but the icy draft revived her and gave her a glimmer of hope. If only they weren't too late!

The pavement near the Fallons' apartment hadn't been cleared of snow, which lay packed and uneven with bits of litter trapped under a sheen of ice, but the place wasn't nearly so sinister when seen from the inside of the car with Dad sitting beside her, and this time they found the right building with no trouble. They could see that the light was on in the Fallons' apartment from the bottom of the staircase, and the door had a cheerful wreath of plastic holly above the letter slot.

"Take my cell phone," said Dad. "Call me at

home when you're ready to leave." He waited in the car long enough to see her walk carefully up the steps with the wrapped-up portrait. She rang the bell. After a few moments the door opened and she disappeared inside. Then he drove off.

When Eve saw what Hannah was carrying, her eyes sparkled with anticipation. She drew her into the apartment, shutting the door behind her, and made her sit down while she tore off layers of brown paper and bubble wrap, chattering all the time. The twins looked up briefly from the cartoon they were watching on TV, then lost interest and looked back again.

"I never really meant to ask for it! What nerve you must have thought I had after you'd put in all that hard work. I never really thought—" She took off the final layer, and Sam's portrait was revealed.

For once in her life, Eve Fallon was speechless.

"Oh, Hannah!" she breathed at last. "It's . . . it's as good as a photo!" She frowned in bewilderment. "What am I saying? It's better than any photo. It's . . . it's more . . . real." Her voice trailed off as she stared at the portrait in astonishment, not able to find the words for how the picture made her feel, and not quite understanding it, either. "My boy. My Sam," she murmured. "Oh, Hannah! Wait till

Arthur sees it! He's going to be so proud!"

Hannah looked up, and her heart gave a little lurch. Eve's normally bright, sparkly eyes were wet and misty.

But she had no time to spare for sentiment. "Where's Sam, Mrs. Fallon?"

"In his bedroom, wrapping up one or two things for—" Eve jerked her head toward the twins' backs and winked. "Go on in. He'll be glad to see you."

As she entered the room, he was kneeling on the floor with a roll of tape in one hand and a small pink-haired doll in the other. He looked up in surprise, and she shut the door behind her.

"We've got to go," she said quietly. "Now. I know where this meeting is."

"Where?" His eyes widened.

"In the place they call the almonry. It's near the cathedral."

"How do you know?"

"Never mind how I know! Just come quickly. I'll explain as we go."

Without another word he got up, picked his jacket off the floor, and left the room with Hannah following.

"We're going out for a bit, Mom," he told his mother casually.

"What, right now?"

"Not for long. There's some people from school doing a bit of carol singing in town."

"All right." Eve looked surprised by this uncharacteristic behavior but mercifully made no objection, and in spite of her agitation Hannah marveled at Sam's ability to lie with such fluency and conviction.

It took longer than she'd hoped to reach the cathedral courtyard. The streetlights only partially dispelled the darkness, and the ground was slippery and treacherous. More than once Sam had to grab her as she stumbled and almost fell. The long illness had made her weak and unsteady, and the effort of trying to talk at the same time exhausted her.

"It was Dad's crossword puzzle that gave me the clue," she told him breathlessly. "It was an anagram, you see. That's why 'normaly' was spelled wrong on the recipe. They'd used a kind of code."

"Hm." He sounded muted.

"What's the matter? Do you think I'm wrong?"

"Don't know. All seems a bit far-fetched some-how."

"But it was you who thought of it in the first place!"

"I know. Now . . . I'm not sure."

"Then what are we doing here?" She looked at him, aghast. He wouldn't let her down now, would he?

He shrugged. "We may as well go to this almonry place now that we're here. What's it used for, anyway?"

"I think the chaplain said the choir uses it for practices."

"Well, that's probably what they're doing right now."

The cathedral lay bathed in floodlights, like a great ship anchored in harbor. They followed the line of the old monastery wall with difficulty, as the stones were now partly obscured by snow, and she had only a hazy recollection of her tour with the chaplain.

But when they reached the low, brooding shape of the almonry, the windows showed only darkness.

Hannah's heart sank.

"Is this it?"

She nodded.

"Are you crazy or something? Who's going to perform satanic rites or whatever in a place like this? Anybody can see in!"

"They could be in the dark," she said defensively, but even as she said it, she knew Sam was right. The whole idea was ridiculous.

"I suppose the door's locked," he muttered, walking down the steps and trying the handle.

But to their surprise it wasn't. As Sam's hand found the light switch, the long, high-ceilinged room was flooded with harsh fluorescence that showed only four rows of chairs, a row of pegs with red choir robes hanging from them, a battered bookcase, and a large brick fireplace. It was exactly as it had been on the day the chaplain showed her around.

"I'm sorry. I was wrong." Hannah's voice was dull with misery.

He switched off the light and they went out, closing the door behind them.

"I guess we should go home. There's no point looking anywhere else now. It's almost six thirty already." Tears of frustration blurred her eyes.

"Wait a minute." His voice was suddenly alert. "Look."

"Where?"

"Look at the chimney."

She looked up and saw, in the faint light coming off the cathedral, a thin column of smoke rising up unwavering into the night sky.

"But . . . there wasn't any fire lit in there, was there?"

He shook his head. "Must be upstairs."

"There isn't an upstairs. Just that one room. Look, there's only a single row of windows."

They both stared at the outside of the building. There were no windows above the ground floor.

"An attic, then."

"There'd have to be stairs leading up to it. I didn't see any, did you?"

"We must have missed them."

He led the way back down the steps and opened the door. Instinctively, they walked quietly across the tiled floor, keeping their voices low. But there was no sign of any stairs, and the fireplace was empty, its grate swept clean.

"There must be another way into this place," muttered Sam. "Let's go back out."

In silence they left the building and walked around the outside, searching carefully in the gloom for a door, but they found nothing. There was no way in other than the door they had used.

"The chaplain said there used to be cellars and storerooms underneath all the monastery buildings," whispered Hannah. "Maybe there's an underground passage leading from . . ." She looked around her, but there was no building nearer than the cathedral itself. "Wait though! I think he said the floor in there is the old one, the original. This place was built on top of it."

"No smoke without fire," murmured Sam. "We'd better go back."

Once more he led her into the empty room and began walking stealthily, staring down at the worn, cracked tiles of the floor.

Hannah was beginning to feel sick. It was as if someone had tied a rope around her stomach and was pulling it tight. She looked at her watch. It said six forty-five. Were they already too late?

Suddenly Sam gave a muttered exclamation. He was down at the far end of the room, crouching over the stone tiles of the fireplace. "Come over here a minute," he said softly. "I found something."

As she joined him, he pointed to four tiles at the back of the grate that formed a rectangle about three feet by two. "See these? The mortar's broken around them. They're not fixed anymore." He reached into his pocket and pulled out a small penknife, inserting the blade between the two back tiles and levering underneath the one nearest him. But it was stuck fast. He tried the end of the tile next to it, which formed part of one side of the rectangle, pushing the knife down hard to clear the mortar. Then he had a shock. The blade of the knife disappeared up to the hilt.

"That's weird! This tile's thicker than the others." He pulled out the penknife and pushed it down the side of the neighboring tile. Again, the blade disappeared immediately. This time, instead of removing the knife, he levered underneath the tile, and then, gradually, before their eyes, the entire rectangular section of fireplace began to move! Trembling with excitement, he lifted it out to reveal an arrangement of wooden planks, dark and brittle with extreme age, that were stuck firmly to the bottom of the tiles.

But where the planks had been, instead of a solid floor, there was now a gaping hole. A hole with rough, uneven stone steps spiraling down into black nothingness.

CHAPTER TWENTY-SEVEN

DESCENT INTO THE CELLAR

For a moment neither of them spoke. Each knew what the other was thinking. Here was the danger they had come to confront. To confront and to challenge. There was no going back now.

"We should call the police," muttered Sam.

"No time," she whispered.

He looked at her. "You up for this?"

The rope around her stomach tightened another notch. She nodded.

"Turn the lights off, just in case. . . ."

But she knew what he meant. Just in case somebody discovered what they were doing and decided to follow them. Anybody could close the entrance behind them so they were trapped down there.

As silently as she could, she walked to the door and pushed the switch upward. The floodlights from the cathedral were now their only help.

Sam took a deep breath and launched himself over the side of the shaft till he was on the top step, looking down. "We'll have to go down backward. Too narrow to risk any other way, and there's nothing to hold on to. I just wish we'd brought a flashlight."

He turned around and began to feel the way with his feet, one hand on the step at head level, the other on the central support of the spiral. She watched until the top of his head was almost invisible in the gloom; then with fast, shallow breathing and a pounding heart, she followed him.

The shadows closed over them horribly quickly, and soon the residual light from the room above had quite vanished. It was pitch-dark, and the smell of damp and mold was overpowering. They had no way of knowing how far the steps went. And no way of knowing what was waiting for them when they reached the bottom. That was if they reached it before whoever was down there discovered them first. . . .

Progress was painfully slow, as Sam kept stopping in an effort to control his fast, panicky breathing. It wasn't quite as bad for Hannah, because she knew that while he was in front of her she was safe for at least those few feet, but she dreaded the possibility of him suddenly losing his balance, or reaching a part of the shaft where the steps simply disappeared into nothingness and he with them. The stone was icy beneath her hands, and it seemed she had been doing this for hours, reaching behind her with one foot, bringing her hands down a level, taking the other foot down to join the first one, then starting all over again. The darkness confused her sense of time and space.

She tried not to dwell on what they expected to find when they reached the bottom of the steps, but her mind was full of sinister images. Scenes of devil worship? Some kind of Black Mass? And what exactly did "witches meet" mean? Two or three, or a whole coven? She shivered.

At last she noticed that for the first time the darkness wasn't quite absolute. It had thinned very slightly to show a vague outline of step and support. Before long she could make out her hands in front of her, and as the light became stronger, she saw that it wavered unsteadily.

Then Sam froze. "Stop!" he whispered.

They had reached a narrow platform beyond

which the steps continued downward, but the shadows that licked the damp, green-stained wall behind warned them that with the next turn of the spiral they could be seen.

Very slowly, Sam steadied himself against the central support and peered around it. Then he rapidly withdrew his head. He beckoned, and with a thudding heart Hannah forced herself to look.

The staircase ended in a long, low-roofed cellar. The fireplace was invisible, as it was below and to the left of the platform, but the shifting, uncertain light it cast showed thick walls with deep recesses stacked high with wooden crates and pallets, mostly blackened and rotting now, as if the room had once been used for storage. Two large metal boxes, half eaten away by rust and with locks hanging loose, were just visible in the gloom, but the corners of the cellar were shrouded in darkness. The huge stone flags of the floor still showed traces of ancient straw, and a pile of sacks lay against the far right-hand wall, ragged at the base with small holes, from which had spilled trickles of grain that had stiffened into dark clumps. Nearby lay what looked like the bones of a small animal.

Other than that there was nothing, and no sound except for the crackle and hiss of the fire.

Whatever they had expected to find down here, it wasn't this.

Suddenly Hannah was gripped by a terrible fear. Abandoning all attempts at caution, she jumped down the remaining steps and ran wildly across the stone floor. Sam followed more cautiously, and together they stared into the charred embers beneath the dying flames. But if the little statue had once been there, no trace of it remained now.

"We're too late! They must have destroyed it already. Burned it and left!"

Sam heard the tremor in her voice but could think of no words to comfort her. The fire and the empty room seemed to make it all too likely that she was right. He glanced bleakly toward the staircase.

Suddenly he frowned. "Listen!"

"What?"

Then she heard it too. A faint shuffling noise, followed by a light tapping, which repeated itself, getting gradually louder. At the same time they noticed a thin, erratic beam of light that descended slowly, becoming stronger as they watched. Someone was coming down the stairs.

Desperately, they looked around for somewhere to hide, but the crates and boxes were too few and too small to keep them concealed for long, especially from someone who, unlike them, had come armed with a light. They stared at each other hopelessly, then turned to the foot of the staircase and braced themselves.

Abruptly the footsteps stopped. The beam of light hovered a few feet above ground, moving very slightly but no longer descending. Now the sudden silence was even worse than the waiting, and Hannah felt her heart knocking painfully against her ribs. What was going on? Then she realized. Whoever it was had stopped on the little platform, just like they had, and was listening.

They stood still, hardly daring to breathe. At last the footsteps began again, and all at once a figure came into view. It was a slight person carrying a pencil flashlight and a canvas tote bag. Hannah heard Sam's sharp intake of breath. A second later she too recognized the gray hair pulled back into a bun, the long nose, the receding chin.

"Miss Murdoch!" she whispered.

Then they both stepped back, shielding their eyes as the glare of the flashlight found them. For a moment nobody moved. At last Miss Murdoch lowered the light.

"Sam? Hannah?" she whispered harshly. "What

are you doing here? Have you any idea what kind of danger you are in?"

Hannah said nothing. She was too shocked to speak, but Sam stepped forward boldly.

"We were hoping you might tell us that."

"What do you mean?" She had stopped whispering, but now she sounded baffled.

"I think you know!"

"Know . . . what?"

"Why are *you* here, Miss Murdoch?"

"I . . . saw the notices, of course."

"Saw them, or wrote them?" His voice was accusing.

Her eyes widened. "What are you suggesting?"

"What have you got in that bag?"

She looked down at the canvas tote bag still in her hand, as though noticing it for the first time. "But . . . you surely can't think?" She stared at him, horrified.

"Let's see then," he said, jerking his head toward the bag.

Slowly Miss Murdoch handed it to him.

He snatched it from her and peered inside. Then he gave a muttered exclamation and turned to Hannah, holding out the bag for her to see.

Shaking with fear and hope, she looked. But

there was no statue, and no tools of witchcraft. The only thing in the bag was a large bottle of the kind used to spray roses for greenflies. A bottle of insecticide.

"It was the only weapon I could find," said Miss Murdoch apologetically. "The instructions warn that if it comes in contact with the eyes, it can cause temporary blindness. Used at close range, I hoped it might disarm whoever was down here long enough for me to prevent whatever mischief was being planned. I suspected that it involved the statue, and I knew that it had something to do with you, Hannah, but I still have no idea of the true nature of that involvement." She pursed her lips and shook her head. "If only I had thought to warn you, I could have prevented your coming here tonight, but I never thought you would figure out the hidden meaning in those recipes."

Hannah looked from the bag to Miss Murdoch, then back to the bag. Desperately, she wanted to believe that what she was hearing was the truth. She looked at Sam, but his face was stern. Then she looked at the teacher and saw the hurt in her eyes.

"Oh, Hannah, you suspected me? You, of all people? I thought you trusted me!"

Hannah looked down at the worn stone floor and blushed with shame.

Now Miss Murdoch stopped looking hurt and frowned. "Does this mean that you have no idea who wrote those messages?" she asked sharply.

Hannah shook her head. "None at all."

"But you knew someone was after you?"

"Yes."

"Do you know what they were looking for?"

"I . . . I think so. Yes."

The teacher took a deep breath, then let it out slowly.

"Hannah, listen to me. Listen carefully. Whatever it is you have, somebody else wants it so badly that they may stop at nothing to take it from you. Nothing. Do you understand me?"

She nodded, eyes wide with fear.

Miss Murdoch's gaze fixed her with a relentless intensity.

"Do you have that thing with you now?"

Before she had a chance to stop herself, Hannah's hand went to the locket. "Yes," she whispered.

CHAPTER TWENTY-EIGHT

THE TRAP

Sᴀᴍ sᴛᴀʀᴇᴅ ᴀᴛ ʜᴇʀ ɪɴ ʜᴏʀʀᴏʀ, and slowly, a sickening sense of dread began to invade her. A trap had been set and she had fallen straight into it. The chemicals in that bottle had been meant for them!

But before any of them had a chance to move, a voice rang out from the far end of the cellar.

"Stop there, Millicent Murdoch. You have gone far enough!"

Wide-eyed, openmouthed, they peered into the shadowy darkness as Mr. Cristanthi walked toward them.

He walked quickly, purposefully. His brown eyes burned with intensity and his mouth was set in a hard line.

The two children drew close together and turned fearfully to Miss Murdoch. Even in the fitful light, they saw that her face was livid with terror. Then she staggered and sank to the ground.

Trembling with shock, Hannah's hand felt the locket.

But now Mr. Cristanthi was kneeling down beside the collapsed woman. He took her hand and seemed to feel for a pulse. At last he straightened up, and for the first time he looked at them. "We must get her to a doctor."

When neither of them moved, he frowned. "Come, she is no threat to you now. Sam, help me to lift her. She will be no great weight. Between us we can get her up the steps, I think."

Reluctantly, Sam moved toward the slumped form. "She doesn't deserve our help," he muttered angrily. "You heard her. She tried to make Hannah feel guilty for not trusting her. And all the time it was her we shouldn't have trusted!"

Mr. Cristanthi nodded somberly. "I have had my eye on her for some time. I knew she was looking for something, but it wasn't until the notices appeared that I realized someone at the school was an object of special interest." He looked at Hannah. "That someone was, of course, you."

"She stole the Child," she whispered. "She's the only person who knows where it is. What if she . . . ?" But she couldn't bring herself to finish the sentence.

"What if she does not recover? That is a risk, of course, but I think that the meeting she called here tonight proves that it is not far away." His eyes roved briefly around the room. "It may well be hidden here, in the cellar. As soon as we can get her upstairs and call an ambulance I will return, and we will search."

"Where are the others?" asked Sam suddenly. "If it was meant to be a meeting, why is no one else here yet?"

"I have no idea," replied Mr. Cristanthi briskly. "But clearly, we have no time to lose." He took an expensive-looking flashlight from his pocket and switched it on. The powerful beam cast a bright light on the ancient, soot-blackened walls and ceiling.

Carefully, he and Sam lifted the slight figure of Miss Murdoch and carried her to the base of the steps.

"Will you be all right by yourself?" Sam asked Hannah anxiously. "We'll be as quick as we can."

She swallowed. "Will you have to go far?"

"I shall call the ambulance from the almonry," replied Mr. Cristanthi reassuringly. "If anybody tries to enter, they will not get past us."

Then she watched as the two of them began slowly to maneuver their awkward burden up the stone staircase. Gradually the light faded until it dwindled to nothing, and she was alone in the empty cellar with only the flickering waning fire for company.

Hannah suddenly felt a numbing tiredness. The tension of the last hour, combined with the shock of Miss Murdoch's betrayal and the sense that the little statue might still be out of their grasp, filled her with a dull weariness. She needed to rest, but there was nothing to sit on. Only the filthy straw with its detritus of centuries-old litter. She peered around for a spot where the stone flags were reasonably clear of mess, and sank down. The cold of the stone seeped into her, chilling her body, her brain.

She began to feel drowsy. The firelight confused her, creating a shifting, shadowy world where nothing was what it seemed. The more she stared at the objects around her, the more she tried to fix them in space and shape, the less certain they became. Then all at once, her senses felt heightened, her mind alert.

The empty crates now looked empty no longer but freighted with strange goods. The pungent smells of spices and fruit, of salted fish, of animal skins, filled her head and made her dizzy. A scuttling sound nearby made her stare at a patch of straw where a bright-eyed rat, its long nose quivering, crept toward a sack of grain. And now the dark shadows near the walls began to shift in a different way, with purpose and definition. They were not shadows anymore but shapes. Hooded, cloaked figures who, as she watched, began to move slowly toward her.

A scream rang out, echoing around the cavernous room. She sprang to her feet in terror, and as the shadows subsided and the nightmare retreated, she heard a voice.

"Hannah! Are you all right?" The voice was solid flesh and blood, and it was accompanied by a light. A wonderfully normal kind of light. Then, just as Hannah thought she might faint from pure relief, Mr. Cristanthi appeared around the bend of the staircase.

"Why did you scream like that?" He ran down the final few steps and reached her side.

"I . . . must have fallen asleep," she muttered. "I thought I saw—" She shook her head, trying to rid it of the images that still made her tremble violently.

"You must sit down," he said firmly. He walked briskly to the side of the room and, after a few seconds, selected two of the sounder-looking crates, upended them, and dragged them over to the fireside. He took a handkerchief from his pocket and attempted to wipe away some of the grime of several centuries so that she could sit down. Then he stepped to the fireplace and carefully placed more logs on the fire from a cardboard box that she now noticed for the first time.

"We will stay here for a few minutes, until you feel strong enough to move," he said, lowering himself onto the crate next to her.

Hannah wanted nothing more than to escape from this terrifying place as soon as possible but knew he was right. Until she stopped shaking, she couldn't go anywhere. "Where's Sam?" she asked.

"I left him to wait for the ambulance. I thought it better to get back to you as soon as I could."

"We must look for the Child," she muttered.

"Of course! But later. There is plenty of time. While we wait for you to gather your strength, we can talk."

She tried to clear her head. There was something

nagging her. "How did you know about the statue? That it was connected to the notices?"

He smiled. "I thought you would ask me that, sooner or later. It was a strange coincidence, you see."

"What do you mean?"

"You and I being in the cathedral at the same time."

"When?" She frowned, trying to remember if she had ever seen him in there.

"The day you drew the statues."

"You were there?"

"There was a storm, wasn't there? An unexpected storm. I don't recall it being forecast."

"No. No, I don't think it was."

"I went there, like you, to shelter from the rain."

Dimly, she now remembered the man with the umbrella. The man who had watched her leave.

"It was cold in there that day," he remarked casually.

She shrugged. "I suppose so."

"But you weren't cold, were you, Hannah? You were warm. So warm you had to take your scarf off."

So he had noticed that, too.

"Then you drew. A perfect image!"

She frowned. How did he know about the

drawing? Had the chaplain told him?

"You drew like one possessed!"

"That's what the chaplain said," she murmured.

"While outside, the lightning flashed and the thunder rolled!"

She nodded doubtfully. Why was he so obsessed with the weather?

"Then I began to wonder," he said thoughtfully, "if you might be acting as some kind of channel."

"A channel?" She stared at him.

"A conduit for the energy of the storm."

"What do you mean?"

"I wondered if it might perhaps be using you to make contact with another kind of power."

"What kind of power?" Her heart had suddenly started to beat faster.

He spoke quietly. "Those statues are of no common oak. The tree from which they were carved was once part of an ancient grove. A wood whose roots reached deep into the past. Centuries before the monasteries and cathedrals were ever thought of, men understood the sacred power of the great tree gods, and sought to propitiate them with blood and sacrifice!"

She looked at him in bewilderment. "But . . . what's any of that got to do with me?"

"As I watched you, it seemed to me that when you drew those figures, you had somehow discovered a way to unlock that power."

She shifted on the hard crate, uneasily reminded once more of Miss Murdoch's words. "The oak was revered above all other trees for its magic and its strength. It is said that when an oak tree is felled, it screams, like a person!"

"You're wrong," she said flatly. "I don't know anything about power. This is a waste of time. We should be looking for the statue."

"So I came to the conclusion," he continued as if she hadn't spoken, "that you must be a witch."

The sheer unexpectedness of this took her breath away. She laughed. "But of course I'm not a witch!" Then a horrible moment of self-doubt crept into her brain. Could she be, without knowing it? Was that the real reason why she'd been able to draw the statues so quickly, so easily? Had she been, somehow, possessed?

But now he was speaking again. "I confess I was intrigued. Occult power is unusual in one so young, but by no means unheard of. I decided to find out more about you." He looked apologetic. "I followed you home."

"You . . . what?" She stared at him in disbelief.

No wonder she'd felt as if someone was behind her!

"As soon as I knew where you lived, it was a simple matter to keep an eye on you. The next day I followed you to the house of the old lady. I sat behind you in the cinema." He smiled. "Then you provided me with the opportunity I needed. You went home with Sam Fallon."

A tiny trickle of fear crept into her then. It felt like icy water. "Sam?" she whispered.

His lip curled slightly. "The people who live in those apartments are used to official visits of one kind or another. The police, the bailiffs, the tax inspectors. . . ."

She held her breath.

He stood up now and regarded her steadily. "Perhaps I should explain. You see, when you left the cathedral that day, you left your scarf behind."

Her heart gave a single warning thud.

"I gave it to the chaplain to keep for you, but not before noticing your name and the school crest. That scarf provided me with an idea. As soon as I saw it, I realized that I knew someone who taught at that school. Someone who also worked part-time in the cathedral. Someone whose sister was a social worker."

Shock forced air into her lungs at last. "Mrs.

Crawford!" she breathed.

She felt as though she had woken from one nightmare only to be plunged straight into another. But this time there was to be no waking up.

Now Mr. Cristanthi was smiling again. He seemed to be enjoying telling his story.

"Her name is Beatrice Arnold. There is no love lost between the sisters—they merely live together through mutual convenience. To make matters worse, when Mrs. Crawford's husband died, he left her a comparatively wealthy woman, and her sister was always jealous of that wealth. That was what made Beatrice such an invaluable accomplice. She will do almost anything for money."

He paused and regarded Hannah with his head tilted slightly to one side. She looked away, trembling. The room felt unnaturally warm.

"The price I offered was a considerable one. The plan I had in mind was bold, and the recompense had to reflect the risks she would be taking. The trouble was, we had very little time. I had no idea how long you would stay with Sam. It was essential that Beatrice act without delay."

Again he paused as if to make sure she was following him. With a shaking hand, Hannah wiped the sweat from her forehead and waited.

"She began by arranging a small . . . shall we say accident? Jane Crawford fell down a flight of stairs, and the shock resulted in a stroke."

"But . . . she might have been killed!"

"Indeed she might," agreed Mr. Cristanthi, nodding speculatively, "which would have made little difference to my plan in the end. You see, the important thing was to get her out of the way for a week or two, a month at most. At least, that was what I thought at first."

Up until that moment Hannah had still held on to the hope that this man was after all a friend. She had clung with the desperation of a sailor grasping a rock in a storm. Now she let go, and the icy water became a torrent.

She tried to force her mind to think clearly. But the voice continued relentlessly, and she could only listen.

"Now we come to the second part of the plan. The one that involved Beatrice in by far the greater risk. The theft of the statue."

"So it was you behind it all," she whispered.

"As soon as Beatrice had rung the hospital, she left her sister and made her way to the Fallons' apartment block. We kept in touch by phone, so I was able to direct her and assure her that you had not left yet. It didn't matter what excuse she made for the visit, just so long as she established an alibi, and in doing so gave herself a chance to invalidate yours by denying that you were ever there."

His smile was cunning, and Hannah realized bitterly just how cleverly she had been framed.

"After that, she had to get to the cathedral in time for the end of the evening service, put on her sister's robe, wrap a scarf around her face to avoid being recognized, and join the other staff in their final duty of checking that nothing had been left behind. It was a simple task to remove the smaller statue while appearing to flick a duster over it, and by the time the others realized that it was missing, Beatrice was on her way to me!"

With a stab of guilt, Hannah remembered how they had suspected Miss Murdoch of exactly the same crime. They had never thought of the sister. No wonder the other chaplains hadn't been able to tell the difference!

The room was now uncomfortably warm, and the atmosphere was thick. It was getting harder to breath. Where was Sam? Why was he taking so long? Desperately, she realized that she had to keep the man talking, if only to gain time.

"Was it Beatrice Arnold who reversed the crucifix?"

He frowned irritably. "She knew that the theft would be reported in the newspapers and couldn't resist adding her own contribution. She risked discovery with such childish vanity. It was sheer luck that the cathedral staff did not see her do it."

She turned away so that he wouldn't see the astonishment on her face. How could this man accuse another person of vanity? She swallowed, and turned back to him. Oh, where was Sam?

"What did you do with the statue?"

He was still frowning. "At this point my plans suffered a setback. You see, as well as being an avaricious woman, Beatrice is clumsy. In separating the baby from the mother, she accidentally dropped it on the cathedral floor. Fortunately, none of the staff noticed, but when we examined it later, we discovered that one of the Child's fingers was missing. It was essential that I have the entire statue. I insisted that we return to the cathedral the following morning to look for it. We pretended to be searching for a lost earring."

"It was you!"

He gave a self-satisfied smile. "I noticed that you too seemed to be looking for something but thought little of it at the time. Besides, I had my new job to start. Beatrice had been in a very good position to recommend me as a temporary substitute for her sister, and with the help of some excellent references, all of which I wrote myself, I was able to convince the principal that I was just what he was looking for. But then, I have always been good at convincing people, you see."

Again he smiled complacently, and Hannah remembered with a shiver just how well he had taken possession of the class. How he had seemed to control their thoughts, their feelings.

The smile faded, to be replaced by a slight frown. "I wanted to teach at the school in order to find out more about you. But at the same time I needed to know more about that statue. I attempted one or two—shall we say . . . experiments."

The word chilled her. "What kind of experiments?" she whispered.

His face darkened. "No matter now. Not only were they unsuccessful, they were corrupted almost as soon as I began!"

She shuddered but couldn't take her eyes off him.

"At last, reluctantly, I was forced to accept the truth. Someone had acquired that tiny fragment of wood, and was using it to control the statue! Then I remembered that you had been in the cathedral the day after the theft. You had been looking for something, and you had found it. I realized then that I had underestimated you, Hannah Price. You possessed a power infinitely greater than I had at first suspected. It was essential that I recover the missing fragment!"

"You . . . wrote that sign?"

"Of course." He seemed to relax suddenly, as if remembering a joke. "I hope you enjoyed figuring it out. The cooking club was a nice idea, wasn't it? You see, I had to make sure the announcement was cryptic enough to avoid general suspicion, but not so obscure that it would elude you. But just in case, I made a point of drawing your attention to the unusual wording."

"You meant for us to read it!"

"Naturally. Who else?" He raised his hands. "I was afraid that you might be unaware of what you had picked up, and it was essential that you understood before you accidentally threw away the fragment, believing it to be rubbish. You would be on your guard, of course, but now I could be certain of your keeping it in a safe place, from which I might eventually retrieve it." He smiled again. "The second notice was of course intended to bring you here tonight. That was why I showed it to Sam Fallon."

The shock of discovering how easily they had fallen into his trap made her weak and faint. Miserably, she closed her eyes. But a tiny stab of doubt pricked her. How could he have known she would bring the finger with her?

He seemed to read her thoughts.

"There was always a risk that you would leave the fragment behind, but I had a feeling that you would be unwilling to let it out of your sight. And then, luckily for me, poor Miss Murdoch quite inadvertently provided me with the information I needed. I'm afraid that when she realized what she had done, the discovery was too much for her. She has a weak heart, I believe." He shook his head sadly.

A sense of bitter remorse overwhelmed her. Millie had been on their side all the time! She was only trying to help. Why hadn't they confided in her instead of obstinately following their own stupid investigation? If they had, she could have told them of her own suspicions. Instead of which, they had let her be drawn into a situation that had threatened her life! What if she didn't recover?

"She was innocent!" she muttered angrily.

"A witch can never be entirely innocent. But in a way you are right. I had little to fear from Miss Murdoch. Her powers are strictly limited. And in any case, it wasn't her I was interested in, Hannah," he said softly. "It was you." He turned away from her, and now his voice seemed to come from a long way away.

"The Virgin and Child were carved in an age when the old magic still lived in the minds of certain wise men and women. Now it is all but forgotten. Yet the gods have not forgotten."

"What?" Her voice trembled. "What have they not forgotten?"

"The sacrifice of human life!"

"What do you mean?" she whispered.

"The man who carved those statues gave his own life so that they might be born. The gods rewarded him by investing his creation with his own spirit. Do you still not understand, child?" He turned to her fiercely, spitting out the words like tiny drops of vitriol. "Those figures were no hoax, no monkish fraud! Their power was real! It was drawn from the roots of the ancient trees that owned the world before men came with their inventions of fire and axes and good and evil, tainting the old magic with the weak-minded foolishness they called religion!"

"The man who made the statues was a good man," she said softly, and even as she spoke, she wondered at her own certainty in knowing it.

"A good man!" His lip curled in contempt. "The human spirit is like the fungus that feeds on the roots of the forest floor. It may flourish for a while, but soon it dies and rots back into the host that briefly gave it life. But while it flourishes," he said, turning to her once more with a smile that froze her, "it may be seduced from the sunlight toward the darkness."

Hannah shivered, despite the warmth of the room, and the cold, relentless voice continued, like foul water seeping from a drain.

"You see, I was fairly certain that a child of your age, had you been aware of your particular gift, would have found the temptation to use it very hard to resist. Especially"—here he smiled nastily—"a child with, shall we say, your rather unfortunate external appearance? Children can be cruel sometimes, can they not, Hannah?"

She bit her lip but said nothing.

"I made enquiries among your friends. I was fairly sure of hearing one or two tales of spoiled homework, spiders appearing in shoes, perhaps even the odd rash appearing suddenly on a formerly flawless complexion? It would have been hard to resist punishing your enemies!"

The redness that suffused her face now had nothing to do with the heat of the fire. Emily's portrait! But she had destroyed it, hadn't she?

Mr. Cristanthi didn't seem to notice her agitation, however. He was intent on telling his story.

"To my surprise, I heard no such tales. No practical jokes, no hint of spite at all. I could not understand it." He shook his head. "I asked more questions. Discreetly, of course, and always with the appearance of having your own interests at heart."

He narrowed his eyes. "At last I began to understand. The power you held was one over which even I, with all my skill, had no command!"

She turned away, trembling, trying to shut out those malevolent eyes, the cruel mouth.

"It was the power of simple charity." His voice was like ashes. "The deadliest weapon in the human armory!"

For a moment neither of them spoke. The only sound was the roar of the flames in the chimney.

At last Mr. Cristanthi roused himself. "Having identified my enemy, I prepared to fight it. Jealousy, suspicion, resentment were my weapons. But I needed help from another child."

"Tabitha!" she whispered. She had suspected her all along. And she had resented her, felt jealous not just of her, but of everyone else in the class. For a while, she had hated them all.

"It does not matter now," he muttered bitterly, more to himself than to her. "The weapons failed. The power of the statue remained with you. Now the fragment of wood was my only hope, and to get it back, I had to resort to cruder tactics than I had used so far."

"You broke into our house!"

He gave a careless shrug.

"A tiresome procedure, but I thought it worth a try."

"You spoiled Sam's portrait! You wrote the note and followed me to the estate, then you waited for me. You and the old lady!"

"Who was Beatrice Arnold, of course." He smiled now. "I couldn't give her much warning—she didn't have a lot of time to draw a few lines on her face and muffle herself up in a scarf. To be frank, I'm surprised you were taken in, but I suppose the fog must have helped."

"And you would have gotten the locket," she said slowly, "only that man stopped you."

For a moment, she saw a strange expression in his eyes. At first, she thought it was anger, but then she realized it was more than that. It was fear.

"The destruction of the painting was not my work," he muttered at last. "It gave me an opportunity, that was all. I wrote the note, and inserted it behind the picture while I pretended to examine it. The rest is true."

"I suppose it was Tabitha," she said dully. But it didn't matter now.

On that occasion he had failed to get the finger. But now, because of her stupid thoughtlessness, he could take it from her whenever he chose.

Then a sudden thought roused her. If that were the case, why had he waited so long? Why had he kept her here, talking endlessly, when all he had to do was to overpower her and take the locket by force? There was no one to protect her now. If it came to a confrontation between the two of them, there was no doubt who would win, so why didn't he just grab it and get it over with?

"Why are you telling me all this?" she demanded.

Suddenly Mr. Cristanthi got up and disappeared toward the back of the room. Peering behind her, she found she could scarcely see farther than a few yards. Why had the place become so dark? A dull panic rose in her chest. It was getting even harder to breathe. And it was so hot! Where was he? She turned around and stared into the gloom at the other end of the room but could make nothing out.

For the first time, she remembered the phone her father had given her to call him from Sam's house. Quickly she drew it from her pocket and switched it on, looking behind her as she did so. With trembling fingers, she wrote on the screen. "HELP ME. UNDER ALMONRY." She keyed in her parents' number. With a thudding heart, she waited.

Then despair flooded her as she read the words: "No network coverage." Of course! There would be no signal so far underground.

She had never felt more alone. Miserably, she sank her head in her hands, stared at the floor, and noticed something. A small, bent piece of white paper lay at her feet, where it must have fallen when she took out her phone. Frowning, she picked it up and read:

GABRIEL JONES (ARCH.)

PRACTICAL ASSISTANCE OFFERED IN ALL AREAS.

NO JOB TOO GREAT.

Then the number on the back that was unlike anything she had ever seen.

There was no point in trying it, of course. No point at all. Even if she were able to get through, the man who had given her that card wouldn't be able to help her. Not now. But she had nothing to lose. With a sense of utter futility, she pressed the digits.

Then something curious happened. Instead of the number she had entered, a series of little stars appeared on the screen, which flashed on and off alarmingly, as if the phone had been given an instruction that it simply couldn't process. After that, the screen went completely blank.

But before she had a chance to wonder at this, she heard a noise from the near end of the room and hastily stowed the phone in her pocket. Mr. Cristanthi was standing at the foot of the steps staring upward through the stairwell. After a few seconds he stopped staring and looked back at her. He walked toward her, and as he approached, her heart seemed to stop. He was carrying something. A tiny, doll-like figure with laughter in its eyes and childish confidence in its outstretched arms. The confidence of utter security. It was the carved wooden figure of a tiny baby.

For a moment, the relief of seeing the little

statue again after all this time was so intense that it replaced everything else. She gazed at it longingly, marveling again at the utter perfection of the crafts-manship; the simple, radiant beauty of the image. Then, quite suddenly, her mind cleared, and she understood why Mr. Cristanthi had waited so long.

The fragment inside the locket could never have been there simply for the taking. The power of com-pletion was hers only, to bestow or withhold of her own free will. Without that act of free will, the Child that lay in the hands of this terrible man would never be his to control. And as she looked into his eyes, she saw that he knew it too.

Certainty gave her strength. She stood up and held out her arms.

"Give me the baby!"

Warily, he took a step backward. Then he spoke, and she heard the tension in his voice.

"Listen, Hannah. Listen very carefully. We have not much time. The chimney is on fire. It was in-evitable, after so many years of disuse. The room above us is already thick with smoke. In ten minutes, perhaps less, it will be impassable. Give me the locket and we will all escape together—you, me, and the Child."

She trembled, trying to convince herself that

he was lying, that it was a trick to make her give him what he wanted, but the acrid, choking smoke was already filling her lungs, and she knew in her heart that he was telling the truth. He had kept her there, talking, because he knew that in the end the ancient chimney could never survive the fierce heat of the fire he had lit. He knew she would have to escape.

"Give me the Child," she whispered.

"You do not understand what I am offering you!" He spoke rapidly, urgently. "With your gift, and mine, we can achieve great things. I can show you the secrets of the great masters. Leonardo, Michelangelo, they knew the mystic power of darkness. It fed their genius, as it will feed yours. Would you turn your back on such a chance, for a lump of lifeless timber?" His voice was soft now, caressing almost. "I can make you famous, Hannah. As great as they. The whole world will know the name of Hannah Price!"

A memory came to her. Of a visit with her father to one of the big London galleries. A whole wing had been devoted to an exhibition of the work of a famous modern painter. She saw the same gallery, this time with her own paintings hanging on the walls. People were walking slowly from picture to picture, murmuring quietly, reverently studying catalogues. She saw herself being interviewed, slim and elegant, but modest, of course. Secure in the knowledge that she was a great artist. One of the greatest in the world.

Then her imagination showed her a smaller room in the same gallery. But here there were no pictures, only a mirror. And as she gazed into the mirror she saw her own face, grown-up and sophisticated now, but with eyes that stared back at her without recognition. They were the eyes of a stranger.

"Give me the Child," she said huskily.

He turned and walked rapidly to the fireplace, and she watched in dread as he dangled the tiny, helpless figure just above the flames. Then he faced her, his eyes glittering in the firelight.

"Think, Hannah. If I drop the statue now, I can be away and up the steps before you have a chance to follow. I can shut the trapdoor behind me and you will have no escape. Will you run to save the Child's life, or your own?"

She stood rooted to the spot, paralyzed by the fear that if she so much as moved, he would carry out his terrible threat.

"Hurry, Hannah, time is running out. It is running out for all of us."

"Give me the statue!" The heat was so intense

now that she swayed, and a new terror gripped her. She couldn't faint, not now!

"Give it to me!" she pleaded with him.

Then Mr. Cristanthi played his final card.

"Remember your mother," he said softly. "Would you have her go to her grave grieving over her only child? The one child remaining to her?"

His words scorched her. How could he possibly know about Tom? Burning, agonizing tears filled her eyes as a new vision swam before her. A vision of her mother's face, lined and hardened with a sorrow that she refused to share. The vision dissolved and faded, to be replaced by another. This time she saw the sad, patient eyes of a different mother, eyes that gazed back into her own with trust. The terrible creature who stood in front of her was asking her to betray that trust.

And as the full realization of the appalling choice he offered flooded her brain, she saw him smile. A smile that seemed to contain the distilled malevolence of centuries of power and greed. A smile that belonged, for the briefest of moments, not to the man who stood before her, but to a figure in the black, hooded robe of a Benedictine monk.

The illusion passed as swiftly as it had come,

but now an iron bar of pure hatred had entered her soul.

"The Child doesn't belong to you." Her voice shook with fear and loathing. "He doesn't belong to me, either. He belongs to his mother. Whatever you do, he will always belong to her!"

"Is that your final answer?"

She stared at him.

"You refuse me?"

"Yes," she whispered.

"Very well, Hannah Price, you have made your choice!"

He flung the statue onto the blaze and raced up the stairs.

"No!" Her scream of terror echoed from wall to wall. She sprang to the fire and plunged her hands into the leaping flames. She scarcely noticed the searing pain as she snatched the statue away and stumbled blindly with it toward the steps. But even before she reached the base of the staircase, she knew it was too late. Seconds after the last footsteps receded and the final shreds of light disappeared, she heard a heavy thud as the trapdoor closed above her and she was alone in the choking, suffocating darkness.

As tears of despair flowed down her cheeks and

dropped slowly onto the Child's head, washing away the soot and ash, she sank to her knees, cradling it in her arms. "It's all right," she whispered softly, trying to comfort it until the last possible moment. "You're safe now. I'll take care of you."

Soon after, a muffled roar could be heard, indicating that the almonry was at last engulfed by flames.

But by that time she was unconscious.

CHAPTER TWENTY-NINE

AFTER THE FIRE

CARLYLE STREET POLICE STATION was having a busy night. Fourteen people had already been brought in drunk and disorderly, nine car accidents had been reported within the last three quarters of an hour, and a search had been mounted for two missing children. And it was still only nine thirty.

Sergeant Bean looked at his watch and thought longingly of home. He hoped his wife had remembered to tape the special Christmas edition of his favorite television show.

The phone rang and he picked it up. "Carlyle Street!" he barked irritably. "What's that? By the cathedral? Righto. We'll look into it. Thank you." He put the phone down and looked around for someone to send, but every available man was fully occupied trying to keep the peace in the police station, to say nothing of the streets outside.

Only Detective Constable Clutterbuck seemed blissfully unaware of the prevailing havoc. He was bent over a lottery ticket, thoughtfully chewing the stub of a pencil.

Sergeant Bean glared at him. "Clutterbuck!"

"Sarge?"

"Get up off your backside, boy—we're going out!"

The worst of the fire had already been put out by the time they arrived at the cathedral courtyard, but the inside of the almonry building was almost completely destroyed, and in the beams from the fire engines' headlights its windows gaped blindly from their blackened casements. The intense heat had melted the snow, and all around was a sea of mud.

"Nobody in there, I take it?" enquired Sergeant Bean, hurrying up to one of the firemen, who was pushing up his helmet to wipe the sweat from his forehead.

"Your guess is as good as mine. All I can say is that if they're still there, we won't find much now."

"Any idea how it started?"

"Chimney caught fire, we think."

"What? You mean someone lit a fire in there?"

"Probably. Kids messing around."

"Kids," muttered the sergeant. He felt deeply unhappy. "We've just mounted a search for a couple of missing kids. Boy and girl. Twelve years old. No sign of them, I suppose?" His voice was hopeful, but his heart was heavy.

The fireman shook his head. "It'll be a while before it's safe to go in there and look. There's no hurry, I'm afraid."

Sergeant Bean nodded miserably. He would have to alert the parents, of course, and even now it was just possible that Hannah Price and Sam Fallon would turn up safe and sound. But a deep-seated instinct told him that they had been in that building; that it was somehow connected with the missing statue. The Fallons had always been trouble-some, of course. But not really bad. Not like some. And that Hannah Price had seemed a nice child. He'd rather taken to her, in fact. He took a large, carefully folded linen handkerchief from his pocket and blew his nose loudly.

CHAPTER THIRTY

SAM'S STORY

HANNAH WAS DREAMING. She dreamed that she was stuck in a chimney, and beneath her someone had lit a fire. She knew that up above, if only she could get to it, was cool, fresh air, but the more she struggled, the more she stuck fast. At last she saw a chink of light and opened her eyes. There, right in front of her eyes, was a hideously blackened, staring face!

"Who are you?" she whispered terrified.

"Sorry." The face retreated slightly. "Just checking to see you were still breathing."

"Sam? Is it . . . is that you?"

"Who do you think? Santa Claus?" He grinned, his teeth flashing white against the grime.

She struggled to sit up and look around her. She

seemed to be in a sheltered spot on the south side of the cathedral, where the huge stone buttresses supporting the great wall protected her from the wind and the snow. Sam was perched on a narrow ledge next to her, and beneath her was a pile of what looked like old drapes that had once been red but were now scorched and soot stained. One or two more had been wrapped around her for warmth.

But now she felt too warm. She loosened the covering so she could breathe more easily and saw beneath it a tiny wooden figure. Memory flowed slowly, like molasses.

"What happened to you? Why didn't you come back?"

He looked unhappy. "I wanted to, but he, Cristanthi, said it'd be better if I waited with Millie while he went back down to you. As soon as we'd got her up the steps and into the almonry, he called the ambulance, and then he disappeared back into the cellar."

Hannah nodded, trying not to remember what had happened next.

"We waited ages! I thought they were never going to turn up. I suppose it was because it's Christmas Eve or something. There were just too many calls for them to deal with. And the snow and every-thing made the roads harder. Anyway, it was about forty minutes before the ambulance arrived. They said they'd been told the wrong place."

"He must have done that! To keep you there for longer!"

He nodded slowly. "I know that. Now. It was him, wasn't it?"

She closed her eyes for a second, then rubbed them wearily. "Yes. He meant for us to figure out those notices. He wanted us to find the cellar. Him and that social worker. She's the one who stole the statue—she was Mrs. Crawford's sister."

He stared at her. "You're kidding! And we thought she was dumb!"

She nodded soberly, and for a few moments nei-ther of them said anything. At last Hannah spoke.

"So what did you do then? After the ambulance came?"

"Ran back to you as fast as I could, of course. But way before I got there, I knew something was wrong. All this black smoke was coming out of the chim-ney. Then once I got closer, I saw the almonry win-dows looked black too. As soon as I got the door open, I realized the chimney must have caught."

She shivered. "Not surprising. I don't suppose

anyone's lit a fire down there in the last five hundred years!"

He looked at her soberly. "I never really thought you'd still be down there. I reckoned the two of you would have got out as soon as you noticed the smoke, but I needed to make sure. Trouble was, once I got inside the almonry, it was like an oven. The smoke was so thick I could hardly see anything. I went back outside and collected snow in my scarf so I could hold it over my mouth and nose, and that was when I saw it."

"Saw what?"

"There was only one set of footprints leading away from the building. A man's."

He glanced up at her, and she saw the fear in his eyes. Now he spoke fast, as if he wanted to rid himself of the memories as soon as possible.

"I managed to crawl to the trapdoor, but it was shut, and the tiles had been put back. By that time the flames were licking around the top of the chimneypiece. I still had my penknife, but the smoke was so thick I could hardly see the gaps in the mortar where I had to lever the tiles up. It . . . it seemed to take me ages, and all the time the flames were getting bigger."

He paused, exhausted by the effort of recall. "At

last I got it open." He looked at her. "That was when the fire really exploded. It was the draft, see. The draft from the cellar. As soon as I opened that door, I heard this deafening roar, and all Hell was let loose!"

Again he stopped. He was breathing hard. "Then something really weird happened. Somebody was in there. Standing next to me. Only he wasn't coughing, or choking like I was. He just stood there. Then he picked me up and took me outside. He laid me down on the snow and put his jacket over me. But in the time it took to get me out, the place was a solid wall of fire. I tried to tell him that you might be down there, trapped in the cellar, but he wasn't listening . . . it was like he already knew, because he just went straight back in there!"

Sam's voice started to shake. "He just walked back in there like it was . . . I don't know . . . like there was no fire at all! The flames didn't seem to touch him!"

"Then what?"

"He came out. He was carrying you. And a pile of choir robes. The ones you're lying on. At first it looked as if you'd got this doll you were holding. Then I saw it had its finger broken off and I realized.

It was the statue." He stared wildly at her. "You should have been on fire, all three of you, but you weren't even scorched!"

Hannah looked away. Her mind had gone numb, and she suddenly felt very tired. "Sam, you know Millie Murdoch had nothing to do with it."

He nodded. "I know. The shock made her pass out, but apart from that, I think the air in the cellar must have been bad. Once we got up into the almonry, she revived a bit. While we were waiting for the ambulance, she told me something."

"What?"

"It wasn't her who noticed your name on the cooking club notice. Not at first. It was someone else."

"Well?"

"Tabitha Trelawney."

"Tabitha?" Hannah's eyes widened. "But I thought . . . Mr. Cristanthi said—" She stopped. Mr. Cristanthi had never actually said that Tabitha was responsible for any of the things she had suspected her of. She had only assumed it.

"We thought she had something to do with it all. I know," said Sam. "Turns out she went to see Millie a few weeks ago because she thought someone was searching your desk and going through your pockets."

"Who?"

"She didn't say. But it seems like Tabitha knew those policemen were in school that day, saw you were missing from class, and noticed you crying in the library afterward."

"So?" Hannah reddened slightly.

"Well, she thought it was pretty unlikely you'd done anything wrong deliberately, and was kind of curious."

"Why didn't she talk to me about it then?"

"She didn't think she knew you well enough. So for the time being she and one or two of those weird friends of hers started to keep their eyes open and see if anything else happened."

"You mean they were—?" Hannah swallowed.

He nodded. "They were looking out for you."

"But I thought she hated me!"

"She thought you hated *her*. Especially when you didn't reply to that invitation. She was hoping to get a chance to talk to you at her party."

"But I never got the invitation! You were there, you saw!"

He shrugged wearily. "It was just a stupid mis-understanding. Too bad—it would have been good to know that someone was on our side."

She looked down, ashamed. She'd assumed that

Tabitha and her friends despised her because of the way she looked. It had never occurred to her that there might be another explanation for the way they'd seemed to watch her so closely. Then a thought struck her.

"Why did Tabitha go to Miss Murdoch?"

"She'd seen the two of you in the staff room, discussing extra tutoring. She must have thought, whatever was going on, you could have talked to her about it then."

Hannah blushed as she remembered thinking that Tabitha would immediately spread the news that Hannah Price was so stupid she needed extra math, when in fact she'd only used the information to try to help.

"I don't deserve any friends," she muttered miserably.

He ignored this remark, and seemed to be puzzling over something. "What I still don't understand," he said at last, "is who put those tiles back. The ones that hid the entrance to the cellar. Cristanthi was already down there, but he couldn't have put them back, not from the inside."

"It must have been Beatrice Arnold," she said slowly. "No one else can have known about it."

"But why? If they wanted us to go down there,

why risk us not finding the entrance?"

"Mr. Cristanthi said that Beatrice Arnold reversed the crucifix on her own. He didn't tell her to do it. Maybe, in the end, she resented the power he had over her, and wanted to do something to mess up his plan, even if it meant that he never got the missing finger. I don't think she really cared about that. She only stole the statue because he paid her to do it, you see."

"We'll probably never know," he muttered. "And by now they'll have had plenty of chance to escape. The police will never catch up with them."

"I guess not." Hannah looked bleakly away.

Then Sam gave a sharp exclamation. He was staring toward the other side of the cathedral close, where a figure was approaching.

"That's him!" he said suddenly.

"Who?"

"The guy who rescued you from the cellar!"

He scrambled off the ledge and ran toward the man, while Hannah's eyes widened in disbelief as a tall, stooping figure carrying a clipboard and wearing trousers far too short for him came shambling toward them.

"Mr. Jones!" she whispered.

THE HEALING OF
THE TREE

Mr. Jones stopped as Sam reached him, and the two of them stood a little way off, talking in low voices.

She couldn't hear what was being said, but she could see Sam's face. And as she watched, she noticed something very unexpected. If she hadn't known Sam so well, she would have said he looked embarrassed. Embarrassed and something else. He looked pleased. As if he were being praised for something. But his face had none of the mocking self-assurance she was used to. And as she continued to watch, she felt a sudden realization. The boy she had drawn, the boy of the portrait, had disappeared. In his place was a new Sam. A Sam who had somehow grown up.

But before she had a chance to consider this, Mr. Jones left Sam and ambled toward her.

"How are you?" he enquired.

"You saved my life," she said slowly.

"Oh, that." He waved a hand airily, as though saving lives were something he did every day. "All part of the job. I got your message, you see."

"But . . . you couldn't have. I mean, I never sent it. And anyway, there was no signal."

"No? Well, believe me, some of the signals I receive are a good deal weaker than that!"

"But how did you get here so quickly?" She remembered the hair-raising journey in the battered old car and shuddered to think of the trail of wreckage Mr. Jones might have left behind him.

"Oh, no problem there," he said vaguely. "I'm used to traveling quite long distances in a remarkably short time."

"Mr. Jones," she said carefully, "what exactly is it that you do? I mean, what is your job?"

He looked thoughtful. "I work for a kind of aid organization," he said at last.

"A charity, you mean?"

"Charity?" He pronounced the word with care, as if considering its suitability. Then he nodded in approval. "Charity. Yes, I like that. In fact, you could say that's why I'm here in the first place."

"But I'm not ill, or poor, or anything like that."

"No, no," he agreed.

Hannah decided they'd played this guessing game long enough. "Mr. Jones, why exactly are you here? I mean, who are you here to help?"

"Well, you of course. Special assignment. Top priority." He held a finger to the side of his nose and nodded importantly. "They sent me because I'm in rather a senior position."

She looked at the shabby, ungainly figure with misgiving. She'd already met one dangerous lunatic that evening and hoped this wasn't going to turn out to be another.

"I think there must be some mistake," she said at last. "I'm not a special assignment. I'm just Hannah Price."

"That's right! That's what it says here." He consulted the clipboard. "Hannah Price. Just underneath the job reference."

"What is the job reference?" she asked, her curiosity overcoming her suspicion for the moment.

"Matthew twenty-five: thirty-five, thirty-six, and forty," he replied promptly.

"That's not a job reference, it's a Bible reference!" She stared in bewilderment. Clearly the man was crazy. A religious fanatic or something like that. But at the same time, a memory came to her. A memory of a warm fire, a heavy cat, and a man with a striped tie knotted around his waist. Matthew, chapter twenty-five, verses thirty-five, thirty-six, and forty. Wasn't that the passage the bishop had made her read?

"'For I was an hungred, and ye gave me meat,'" she muttered as the words came back to her. "'Thirsty, and ye gave me drink.'"

"'I was a stranger, and ye took me in: Naked, and ye clothed me: I was sick, and ye visited me: I was in prison, and ye came unto me.'" Mr. Jones finished off the quotation cheerfully. "Excellent! You know the passage. That's quite unusual nowadays."

Hannah shook her head impatiently. "Mr. Jones, please believe me, there's been some mistake. I've no idea what this is all about, only that it's got absolutely nothing to do with me!"

Again he consulted the clipboard. "Let me see. Ah yes. Here it is. 'Brown, Katie. Age eleven. Recipient of one coat with hood attached, one item of confectionery from the planet Mars, and a can of cocoa.'"

"Coke," murmured Hannah.

"I beg your pardon?"

"It was Coke. Not cocoa."

"Dear me. Clerical error. Scribes getting slack, I'm afraid." He frowned and made a note on the sheet.

"Anyway, to continue. 'Wainwright, Jessica. Age twelve. Invited to a cinematic entertainment.'"

"A what?"

"*Space Warriors*," said Mr. Jones, peering at the clipboard. "That mean anything to you?"

"That was the movie we went to see. Me and Sam. And Jessica. She was new, you see. She hadn't had time to make friends."

"Exactly! She was a stranger, and you took her in."

"But that's ridiculous!" Hannah shifted uncomfortably on her bed of choristers' robes. "We just took her along to the movie, that's all. And Katie had lost her coat, so I lent her mine. I bought her a Mars bar and a drink because she didn't have any money. Anybody would have done the same thing!"

"Perhaps," replied Mr. Jones. "But you *did*, you see."

"In any case, I don't know anyone who's sick," she went on rather desperately. "And I've definitely never visited anyone in prison. I keep telling you, it's all wrong. Mistaken identity or something."

But Mr. Jones had returned to his clipboard.

"'Abbott, Edith. Age seventy-four. Currently under house arrest. Visited regularly since March of last year.'"

Hannah almost laughed with relief. "There you are, what did I tell you? It's a mistake! Mrs. Abbott's not under house arrest, she just can't go out. She's got agra . . . agra . . ." Why could she never remember what it was called?

"Agoraphobia," supplied Mr. Jones, consulting his clipboard again. "It's a kind of sickness. 'Agora' means an open space. 'Phobia' means fear. From the Greek," he added helpfully.

"Yes, but—" she began, then stopped as she remembered Mrs. Abbott's sour, unhappy old face. Where was she if not in a prison of her own invention? She needed no locks, no chains.

"I still don't really understand," she said, sighing and shaking her head.

"Don't you? Never mind!" Mr. Jones smiled happily. "It doesn't make the slightest difference whether you understand or not. The point is, what you did was accepted."

"Accepted?" she asked, frowning. "Who by?"

But before he could answer, they were interrupted by the approach of two sets of footsteps, crunching loudly in the snow. D.C. Clutterbuck wore his habitual expression of vacant contentment, but Sergeant Bean was smiling broadly for the first time that day.

"There you are! We've been looking for you two ever since your parents called to say you hadn't come home. Is this your idea of carol singing?" He looked at Hannah with concern. "Are you all right, young lady?"

She nodded.

"And that, if I'm not mistaken, is Sam Fallon." He jerked his head in the direction of the boy standing a little way off.

Sam approached reluctantly, and the sergeant regarded his filthy face and clothes severely. "It's a little early to be coming down chimneys, isn't it?"

"I wasn't in the chimney," Sam said coldly. "I was in the almonry when it caught fire."

"Yes, well, we'll discuss the fire later," said the sergeant hurriedly. "The main thing now is to—"

He broke off as he noticed something Hannah was holding. A wooden doll, it looked like. Only it wasn't a doll.

"That's not . . . is it?" He stared in disbelief. "You had it? All the time?"

"No!" she said indignantly.

Then Mr. Jones stepped forward. "These children are not guilty of stealing the statue," he said. "They simply had the wit to discover where it was hidden."

Sergeant Bean bristled at this slight on his professional competence.

"And, incidentally, the courage to save it," added Mr. Jones mildly.

"It's still broken, though," said Hannah sadly. "I've got the missing finger, but it will have to be stuck on somehow. It won't ever look quite the same."

She glanced down at the little figure in her arms and blinked. Then she rubbed her eyes. Sam, Sergeant Bean, and D.C. Clutterbuck looked curiously to see what she was staring at.

Ten tiny, perfect fingers stretched out toward the night sky.

"Who fixed it?" Sam stared wildly at Mr. Jones.

But the tall man simply smiled and said nothing.

Sam turned to Hannah, but she wasn't looking at him. She was gazing down at the statue, gently stroking the tiny finger, noticing its soft, green, sapling newness. She felt suddenly content. The connection was complete at last. On this magical night the ancient tree had healed itself.

"It is time to take these children to the hospital," said Mr. Jones firmly. "They have both inhaled a great deal of smoke. After that, you must take them to the cathedral. They need to be there before twelve."

"And on whose authority do you give orders around here?" demanded Sergeant Bean.

Then Detective Constable Clutterbuck made his first and last intelligent remark of the evening.

"Sarge," he said slowly, scratching his head, "I don't think he's the kind of guy you argue with."

CHAPTER THIRTY-TWO

EMERGENCY ROOM

AT FIRST IT SEEMED that all those drunk and disorderly people who had begun the evening at the police station had ended up in the emergency room of the city hospital. Several people were wandering around in a dazed condition, nursing wounds of various kinds; one man had blood coming from the side of his head, another was lying on a stretcher with a broken leg, and a woman who had fallen on a patch of ice was proudly showing off an impressive black eye.

Sergeant Bean tried to get Hannah and Sam to sit down while he told the nurse at the reception desk that they needed attention, but to his surprise they edged past him and got there first.

"Millicent Murdoch?" he heard the nurse say above the din. "She went home about ten minutes ago. Are you Sam Fallon?"

"Yes," he shouted.

"Can you give her a call on this number?" She handed him a piece of paper. "She sounded anxious about you."

"Okay."

Sam fought his way through the crowd to a pay phone in the corner of the waiting room and searched his pocket for coins.

Then quite a lot of people simply left.

As they watched, the man who had had blood coming from the side of his head suddenly realized that it wasn't bleeding anymore and discharged himself without a word to anybody. The woman with the black eye found she no longer had an audience because she no longer had a black eye, and the man with the broken leg got up off the stretcher and walked steadily out the door. One by one, the waiting patients left peacefully, until the reception area contained only Sam, Sergeant Bean, D.C. Clutterbuck, and four nurses.

"Was it something I said?" the nurse at the reception desk asked Sergeant Bean.

"I've no idea," he replied, "but I'd like someone

to take a look at these two children so I can get back to the station." He pointed to where Hannah had been standing, but she had disappeared.

Hannah walked quickly down the corridor, turned right at the end, and got into the elevator. When she got out, she walked through a set of double doors and turned right through an entrance that said "Willow Ward."

Unlike the previous occasion, there was a cheerful buzz of chatter coming from the beds.

"I've come to see Mrs. Crawford," she told the nurse on duty at the desk.

"She's feeling a lot better. Do you want to talk to her?" She indicated a little group of armchairs at the end of the ward, where Mrs. Crawford could be seen talking animatedly to a lady in a pink bathrobe.

"No, that's okay," replied Hannah smiling.

"We've got her sister, though," said the nurse helpfully, as though offering a suitable alternative. "A Miss Arnold. She was admitted a couple of hours ago. Very severe stroke, I'm afraid."

She shook her head sadly, but Hannah had already left.

❖   ❖   ❖

Some time later Sir Giles Hunter-Smith, senior hospital administrator, stood in the geriatric ward and regarded the junior resident doctor with disfavor.

"Now let me get this quite straight," he was saying. "What you seem to imply is that whereas at nine thirty this evening there was no free bed, and those that were occupied contained some who were not expected to last the night, now—at eleven o'clock—we have a hospital full of patients who are all—except one—perfectly fine. Is that what you are trying to tell me, Mason?" His eyes glinted dangerously.

The junior resident nodded helplessly, so Sir Giles continued, his voice growing icier by the second.

"And I suppose you are also going to say that old Mrs. Gittins, ninety-four if she's a day, and in a coma for the last eight months, is sitting up in bed and singing Christmas carols. Is that what you're going to tell me, Mason? Well, speak up, man!"

"No, Sir Giles. Not exactly," replied the junior resident truthfully.

Sir Giles stepped forward and opened the door that separated them from Mrs. Gittins.

Andrew Mason had been quite right—Mrs.

Gittins wasn't singing Christmas carols. She was enjoying a nice conversation and a glass of sherry with her daughter and son-in-law.

"Compliments of the season to you, doctor!" she called merrily, as Sir Giles clutched weakly at the bed rail. "Let me be the first to offer you a glass of Christmas cheer! You look as if you could use it— you're not looking at all well, doctor." She looked at him, then, seizing the sherry bottle, filled a plastic hospital mug to the brim and offered it to him with a steady hand.

"Thank you," he croaked hoarsely, sitting heavily on the side of the bed and downing the contents in a single gulp.

The noise in the men's surgical ward was deafening. Nurse O'Connor walked unsteadily between the beds, refilling mugs with champagne. "How many bottles did you say you brought in for the staff this evening, Nurse?"

"Two!" yelled Nurse Reilly.

"And how many glasses have you had out of yours?"

"Thirty-nine! How about you?"

"Forty-six!"

They stared mistily at each other. "Funny,"

murmured Nurse O'Connor to herself. "Reminds me of something. . . ."

Sergeant Bean looked at his watch. Only another three quarters of an hour and he'd be on his way home to his TV show (provided his wife had remembered to record it).

But it was to be some time before the sergeant enjoyed it.

Hannah reappeared in the reception area just as the cathedral clock was striking the quarter hour. "What time is it?" she asked urgently.

"Quarter past eleven," replied Sergeant Bean with satisfaction.

"Quick! We've hardly got any time left! We've got to be back in the cathedral before midnight!"

The sergeant's jaw dropped in disappointment, but he was not a man to shirk his duty, so in less than a minute he, D.C. Clutterbuck, Sam, and Hannah were in the police car and on their way back to the cathedral.

But before they had gone more than a hundred yards, Hannah put a hand on the policeman's shoulder. "Wait!" she said. "Can you turn left here, please?"

"That's not the way to the cathedral," he objected.

"I know. There's somewhere we need to go first. Right at the end of this road, that's it, then left again, and right at the traffic lights. This is it. Heliotrope Gardens. Can you pull over by that house with the silver Christmas tree and all the colored lights?"

Hannah got out of the car. A life-size illuminated reindeer stared glassily at her from the lawn of number 45, but number 43 was in darkness. She pushed open the gate, ran up the path, and knocked loudly on the front door.

"Mrs. Abbott! Mrs. Abbott!" she shouted through the letter slot. "Get up! Please!"

At last she heard footsteps and an irritable voice.

"Who's that waking me up at this time of night? I've been asleep the past two and a half hours!"

"Please, Mrs. Abbott, it's me, Hannah Price! You've got to get dressed and come to church!"

An outraged silence followed; then:

"I haven't left this house in twenty-five years, and I'm not leaving it now, Hannah Price! You go home and let me get back to bed!"

"Just open the door, please, for a moment!" Hannah's voice was desperate. What time was it?

At last came the sound of the chain being reluctantly slid across, and Mrs. Abbott appeared wearing an old bathrobe and looking extremely irritated.

"Well, what is it?" she demanded.

Then she caught sight of the statue in Hannah's arms and she stood quite still. Slowly, very slowly she reached out a hand and touched the baby's head.

"Can you let me have five minutes?" she asked in a voice Hannah had never heard before. Then she disappeared.

While Hannah waited, fretting impatiently, it occurred to her that as she was about to go to church, she should probably comb her hair first. She hadn't done it since this morning, which seemed about ten years ago. A lot had happened since then. A small gilt-framed mirror hung in the hall, the light from the ugly chandelier glimmering disapprovingly on its mottled surface. She glanced warily at her face and suddenly gaped in astonishment.

Her skin was perfectly clear. Not a pimple in sight.

But before she had a chance either to consider this or to comb her hair, Mrs. Abbott reappeared wearing an ancient fur coat that clearly hadn't seen the light of day for a very long time. Hannah took her arm and led her to the waiting police car, where she was installed on the backseat between the two children.

"What's that powerful smell, Sarge?" asked D.C. Clutterbuck after a few minutes.

"Mothballs," replied the sergeant shortly.

The young constable, overwhelmed by the effect of Mrs. Abbott's coat on top of all the excitement, turned pale and closed his eyes.

CHAPTER THIRTY-THREE

THE RETURN OF THE STATUE

MIDNIGHT MASS WAS ALREADY well under way when the strange little procession walked through the west door of the cathedral. Mrs. Abbott came first, trailing essence of mothballs like clouds of incense as she progressed up the aisle. Sam was next, his blackened face making him look like someone about to audition for the part of a Victorian chimney sweep; then came the two policemen, the young constable still unsteady and weaving dangerously from side to side. Hannah was last, cradling the little statue in her arms.

Sergeant Bean grabbed hold of D.C. Clutterbuck's sleeve and sat him down firmly in a pew near the back, taking a seat next to him. "Take your hat off when you're in church!" he muttered, roughly

334

pulling off the constable's helmet and dropping it on the seat beside him. The slight disturbance caused people to turn around, and that was when some of them noticed what Hannah was holding.

The congregation began to look like a field of corn blowing in a light wind. One by one, heads turned toward the central aisle, and a murmuring started that gradually grew louder and louder until the bishop noticed that something was going on, and paused halfway through the absolution to see what it was.

The murmuring stopped, and every eye was on Hannah as, slowly and confidently, bearing the statue before her, she walked forward to the bottom of the chancel steps, turned left along the north transept, and came to a halt at the statue of the Virgin Mary.

It was ten minutes to twelve on Christmas Eve when Hannah carefully fitted the Christ Child into His mother's arms, and the faint click of wood on wood was perfectly audible in the profound hush that wrapped itself around the waiting, watching congregation.

For a moment the city stood still.

Then Hannah turned away and slipped into the end of the second pew from the front, next to Sam and Mrs. Abbott, and the people turned toward the bishop, breathlessly waiting to see if he would stop the service.

But the bishop saw no reason to stop; indeed, he had before his eyes the best reason in the world for going straight on with it. So, with tears pouring down his cheeks, quite unable to read a word and having to trust his memory, he raised his voice, which shook a little, and continued.

When the service was over, the congregation lost no time in crowding around the statues, chattering excitedly. The noise was deafening, and soon it was impossible to see the figures for the throng of people eagerly feasting their eyes on the Child they had thought lost forever.

No one noticed the old man standing a little apart from the crowd, his feet bound in strips of cloth to which sawdust still clung, his blue eyes shining with the age-old brightness of distant stars. Had they seen him, they might have noticed that after a few moments, he simply dissolved into the stone of the pillar behind him.

The bells rang out loudly and merrily across the snow as the congregation at last began to leave. The bishop was waiting for Hannah by the west door.

He took her hands in both of his, and she could feel him trembling. "I had almost given up hope," he said.

"So had I," admitted Hannah. "But you promised me help, and I did get it, you know."

"You did?" He looked mystified. "Well, what of ambition now, Hannah? The statue is back where it belongs, you have already achieved great success in a painting competition, I hear, and, if you don't mind my mentioning it, you seem quite flawless of complexion and rather, er, slighter than when I saw you last."

"That's because I've had the flu. It probably won't last, I'm afraid!"

"Then, as I recall, there was just a problem with math."

"You know, I've been thinking about that," she said slowly. "If I'd been good at math, I wouldn't have had to have extra tutoring, and we wouldn't have known for certain that Millie was a witch, and then we might never have figured out that last message from the cooking club."

He looked thoroughly baffled now. "Clearly I have much to learn. Will you come and see me soon, and tell me all about it?"

She nodded.

❖　❖　❖

Later that night, Hannah sat in bed with the light on. An envelope lay on her bedside table. A letter had been delivered by hand earlier in the evening, but she was too tired to read it now. It could wait till morning.

Gradually, she allowed her mind to wander over the last few months, especially the day that had just gone by: that immeasurably long Christmas Eve. Some things she couldn't yet bring herself to dwell on, or even acknowledge. That would take time. Maybe a lifetime.

Her parents had been so overjoyed to have her back that they hadn't pestered her with questions, but she knew that tomorrow she must give them some account of what had happened in the past weeks, but not a complete account. There was only one person she could trust with the whole story, and that was Sam.

But that could wait too.

Suddenly she was startled out of her thoughts by the sound of the door slowly opening. Her skin prickled. What now? Surely no more could happen to her tonight!

But it was only her mother.

"I'm sorry, Hannah. I saw your light was on. I

should have waited till the morning, but I knew I wouldn't sleep until I'd talked to you!" She sat down on the bed, and Hannah saw that her eyes were red rimmed, her face pale and drawn.

"What's the matter?" she asked. "I'm sorry I gave you such an awful scare, but I'm okay now, honestly."

"It's not that," she whispered. "It's this!" And she produced a battered, light-green folder.

Hannah gazed at her mother in anguish. What a fool she'd been not to hide it properly! Mom could have found it anytime . . . and now it was going to ruin her Christmas. "I'm sorry," she breathed help-lessly. "I never meant for you to see that."

"It's not your fault. I found it when I was search-ing your room today for something that might give us a clue to where you'd gone." She carefully opened the folder and slowly, lovingly, took out each of the drawings in turn, holding them as if they were infi-nitely precious—reexamining them, peering closely so that she didn't miss a single, tiny detail. At last she came to the final picture. The four-year-old Hannah's first attempt.

"It's him, isn't it?" she whispered.

"Yes. It's him." Hannah's voice broke and tears ran unchecked down her cheeks as she watched her mother in an agony of remorse. "I'm sorry, so sorry. I wanted to share him with you, but I never dared. I thought it would only make you more unhappy. And now it has!"

Her mother looked beyond her, as if trying to capture something distant. "I could never see him," she murmured. "That was the thing I couldn't bear! I had no picture, even in my imagination. It's hard to grieve for someone you can't see."

She turned back to Hannah. "Don't you understand? You've given him back to me. This is what I've always been searching for. Now, at last, I can let him go."

And now she wept. For the first time in fourteen years she wept as though her heart were breaking. Breaking afresh, so it could be mended again. But the right way this time.

Hannah put her arms around her mother and hugged her hard.

CHAPTER THIRTY-FOUR

THE BISHOP AND MR. JONES

THAT NIGHT WAS COLD and bright and very still.

Arthur Fallon lay on the narrow bed that was one of the few items of furniture in his small cell, and contemplated his future. When he got out in the spring, he'd see if a garage would take him on as a mechanic. He'd always been good with cars. Wasn't he the one chosen to drive the getaway vehicle last time? Well, maybe that hadn't been such a success. Come to think of it, he'd never had much success at this game. It was time to make a fresh start before Sam and the twins came to think of him as an all-time loser. He'd tell them of his new plans when the family came to see him tomorrow.

❖   ❖   ❖

Sam and Eve Fallon sat in the cozy front room of the apartment, sipping cocoa. The twins had been tucked into bed for hours, identical mock velvet stockings looped hopefully over the bedposts. A plate of cookies sat between them, but Sam for once hadn't touched any.

"All I can say is all's well that ends well," said Eve. "Though what the two of you thought you were doing, traipsing round the city on Christmas Eve looking for statues and I don't know what and giving your parents the fright of their lives *and* getting into trouble with the police, is more than I can say. I've had enough of that sort of thing from your father!"

"Sorry," said Sam.

"I should hope you are sorry! There's Hannah, not even over the flu! She could have come down with pneumonia, and then what kind of Christmas do you think her poor parents would have had?"

"Mm."

"I mean, if it had been a real baby, I might have understood, but a statue! I know it's old and all that, but it's only a bit of wood!"

He said nothing.

"You all right, dear? You don't seem yourself. Exhausted, probably. Time for bed now. You can sleep in as long as you want in the morning."

Mrs. Abbott sat up in bed with a mug of hot milk, happily planning all the things she meant to do in the New Year. She would visit her sister, whom she hadn't seen for fifteen years, ever since the quarrel that had been such a long time ago she couldn't now remember what it had all been about. And she would go to the January sales and buy herself a new coat. One that didn't smell of mothballs.

Millicent Murdoch sat in her kitchen and regarded the little bottle of pills. As she shook out two into her hand, she considered. Was it time to give up witchcraft altogether? They had all had a lucky escape that day, but next time . . . who knew? Perhaps she should wait a little longer, just in case.

She glanced at the clock and noticed irritably that it had stopped again. As soon as Christmas was over, she must get it fixed.

Sergeant Bean snored sonorously on the sofa in front of the special Christmas edition of his favorite show, which his wife had fortunately remembered to record, but of which he had managed to watch only the first five minutes before falling into an uneasy slumber and dreaming that he was trying to rescue D.C. Clutterbuck, who was wearing his helmet above an ankle-length fur coat and being pursued by a vicious-looking illuminated reindeer.

At a little after three o'clock, with the snow thick and freezing hard where it lay, the bishop left his wife sleeping, took a flashlight from the kitchen table and a key from a hook by the back door, and made his way carefully across the courtyard to the cathedral.

He let himself in through a side door and walked slowly down the south transept until he reached the spot where Jacob Martin's figures stood, just where they had been placed on that long-ago Christmas Eve.

With surprise, he realized that he was not alone. A man in a shabby, badly fitting suit was sitting on the altar steps; come in to get relief from the cold, most likely. He wondered vaguely how the man had got in but hadn't the heart to turn him out on this freezing night, and for some minutes they remained in silence, sharing the sense of friendliness that seemed to flow from the small couple.

Then the man stood up. And now it could be seen that he was immensely tall. But his height was nothing compared with the intense, blinding radiance that surrounded him.

The bishop covered his face with his hands and sank to his knees, trembling with fear.

"Why are you afraid?"

The voice wasn't exactly loud, but it seemed to rock the very foundations of the cathedral. "You sent for me. Why should you wonder that I came?"

"I?" The bishop spoke in the merest whisper. "I summoned you? The great archangel himself?"

"Jacob Martin created these figures with love and compassion," replied the voice. "He waited more than six hundred years before a little girl showed herself worthy to continue his work, to restore the power to his statues by offering her own life as he had offered his. You requested protection for that child. Did you imagine your prayers went unheard? *Were you so unbelieving?*"

The bishop could not speak.

"Now, be comforted," said the voice gently, "for through you, tonight the debt is redeemed, and the Child restored."

When the bishop at last raised his eyes, the angel was gone.

CHAPTER THIRTY-FIVE

THE FINDING OF
HANNAH PRICE

IT WAS MORE THAN TWO HOURS since her mother had left, but Hannah was wide-awake.

She lay in the dark, her mind too active for sleep. At last she gave up and, switching on the light, noticed the letter on her bedside table, still unopened.

She sat up and propped herself against the pillows. If she couldn't sleep, she supposed she might as well read something.

Taking the envelope from the table, she eased open the flap with her thumb and took out a single sheet of paper, closely handwritten on both sides. The ink was smudged, and the writing was messy, with much crossing out.

Frowning slightly, she read.

Dear Hannah,

By the time you've finished reading this letter, you're not going to want to speak to me ever again. I should have come to see you after you were sick and told you all this face-to-face, but I wasn't brave enough.

So here goes.

You may have guessed by now that it wasn't Tabitha who searched your pockets and your desk. It was me. Mr. Cristanthi told me he'd seen you in the cathedral the day after the theft and you were looking for something on the floor. Something small, he said. He tried to persuade me that the Child must have gotten damaged when you stole it. Yes, Hannah, he told me he suspected you of stealing it! He said the police suspected you too, and that if we could only discover that you had the missing piece, we could confront you with it and make you put the statue back without anyone else knowing. That way, he said, no one else but us would ever realize who the thief was and you wouldn't get into trouble. And the awful thing is, I didn't believe him! Not really. I knew you'd never do a thing like that.

I expect you're thinking I must have gone

crazy. In a way you're right. I was crazy. Crazy with jealousy. You see, Hannah, I wanted to punish you for being so good at drawing. It's all I've ever really wanted to be good at, and I knew however hard I tried, however much I practiced, I'd never, ever be as good as you. You had the gift and I didn't. It was as simple as that.

It wouldn't have been so bad if you'd been a show-off, bigheaded about it. Then I think I could have forgiven you. Does that sound even crazier? Probably. You see, I'm trying to explain myself. And it's hard because I know that with every word I write, you must be hating me more and more.

Well, it gets worse. You remember Tabitha's party? The one you didn't get invited to? You were invited, of course. But I got to the classroom before you and took your invitation. I wanted you to feel like me. Eaten up with jealousy and anger so you'd do something mean to Tabitha in revenge. You didn't, of course. You're not like that. That's me, not you. I thought I could punish Tabitha, too, because her folks have so much money she'll never need to work for a living. It seemed too good a chance to miss. Two birds with one stone.

Okay, now this is the worst bit. You thought it couldn't get any worse? Well, it can.

It was me who ruined your portrait. Sam Fallon's portrait. I was by myself in the art room the day it was due to be sent off for judging. There it was, Sam's face, smiling at me, mocking me. So perfect. He was your friend. He deserved to be punished, and so did you. I'd seen you making Halloween masks. Everyone wanted one! Because they were so funny. So clever. It was easy for you, wasn't it? You didn't even have to think about it. It just came naturally. Well, now was my chance to turn Sam Fallon's face into a stupid, grinning Halloween mask! The paints were there, all ready for me. Like a gift. One more chance to hurt you. To punish you for having something I can never have.

I don't know if I'm going to have the courage to deliver this letter. Maybe I will, maybe I won't. If I don't, there's a good chance you'll never find out about who searched your things. Tabitha might tell, because she saw me, but somehow I don't think so. You see, she's not like that either.

No one saw me take the invitation, so I'm

*safe there. And no one saw me spoil the paint-
ing. I could just keep quiet. That way I can start
next term by trying to make it up to you.*

*But if I deliver this? Could you forgive me?
I don't think so. Not even you could accept
someone who'd done all those hateful things. I
know I couldn't.*

*If I do manage to get this letter to you, will
you ever be able to understand that however
much you hate me for it, it can never be as much
as I hate myself? Not just for the things I've done
to you and to Sam and to Tabitha, but for what
I've lost in the process. The chance to start
again.*

The chance to be a decent friend, Hannah.
Your friend,
Emily Rhodes

Slowly Hannah refolded the letter and returned
it to the envelope.

For a brief moment she felt angry. Hurt. Then
resentment quickly gave way to sheer amazement,
and she almost wanted to laugh. Emily Rhodes;
beautiful, clever, popular Emily Rhodes had been
jealous of a fat girl with acne who couldn't do math

to save her life! How ridiculous was that? She smiled to herself.

Then she stopped smiling, as astonishment was replaced by a new feeling.

Poor Emily! It must have cost her a lot to write that letter. There had been no instruction to keep it secret. She would have known that she, Hannah, could expose her to the whole school. But somehow she knew that Emily trusted her not to do that. And that was why she wanted to be her friend.

At last she turned off the light and lay down. She had had quite enough surprises for one day.

Suddenly she felt relaxed and happy. There were still ten days of the Christmas holiday left. And the forecast was for more snow. The day after tomorrow she would call Sam and arrange to go sledding. They could even take Emily with them. And Susie of course. And that new girl, Jessica. Tabitha might like to come too.

As sleep overtook her at last, she reflected that maybe it wasn't so bad being Hannah Price after all.

ACKNOWLEDGMENTS

I would like to thank the following people for their support during the preparation of this book: My agent, Eunice McMullen, for believing in it; my editor, Katherine Tegen, for her endless patience in helping me revise the manuscript; my sister-in-law, Ros Coward, for giving her time so generously in the early stages; my dear friends Sally and Fred Shaub, Shuna and Andrew Watkinson, and Carol and Torbjörn Hultmark for their enthusiasm and encouragement when it looked like a hopeless cause; and my family, who had to live with me while I wrote it. I would also like to thank Terry Jacob for checking the basic math in chapter two—the confusion is all my own. Finally, my gratitude to Jeremy Hutchinson, who provided me with the inspiration for the story.

—R.W.

REBECCA WADE

was born in Worcestershire, and much of the research for this book was done in the Worcester cathedral. She is a professional viola player, primarily with the Philharmonia Orchestra in England. This is her first book. She lives in London with her two children.